The Body of Love

Edited by
Tee Corinne

Banned Books ✷ Austin, Texas

A Banned Book

FIRST EDITION

Published in the United States of America
By Edward-William Publishing Company
#292, P.O. Box 33280, Austin, TX 78764

ISBN 0-934411-52-2

"Milk by Susan Stinson previously appeared in *Quickies: Lesbian Short-Shorts*, edited by Irene Zahava, Violet Ink, Ithaca, NY, 1992; used by permission of the author.

"Dimensions" is excerpted from the erotic collection *Seasons of Erotic Love* by Barbara Herrera, Paradigm Publishing Company, San Diego, CA; used with permission of the author and publisher.

A different version of "That Second Wind" by Coleen Carmen was published in *Yoni*, Vol. 3, #1, Winter 1988/89.

Contents

Introduction

Dreams Of The Woman Who Loved Sex, my first book of erotic fiction, was published in 1987. I spent three years trying to find a publisher willing to handle the manuscript. One agent said she thought she could do something with it if I put in some s/m sex. One publisher said it was nice to know what I was doing, but the material was not very erotic. The novella which comprises the major part of the text contains, by design, fifty percent sex. The title prose/poem has, since, been reprinted in several mainstream erotica collections. *Dreams Of The Woman Who Loved Sex* sold out its first print run in six weeks, was #1 on the *Washington Blade* 1987 women's bestseller list and continues to sell competitively.

One of my goals in writing *Dreams* was to gather words, to explore sexual language from a woman-centered point of view. Another was to have a reflection of my life to share with others who might find echos of it in their own lives. *Lovers*, my second volume, asked and answered questions about who is allowed to be sexual in print and about the structure of erotic writing.

I wanted more, though. I wanted a dialogue with other writers working in similar territory and I wanted a broadening of participation, so I edited *Intricate Passions*, which won a Lambda Literary Award, *Riding Desire*, and *The Poetry of Sex, Lesbians Write The Erotic*. I believe that if each of us tells the truths about our own lives and dreams, we will have a literature rich in experience and imagination.

Poet Judith Barrington, in *An Intimate Wilderness*, wants writing about a "sexuality that reveals what it might be, what it will be, when both language and life can unequivocally celebrate lesbian experience." Philosopher Marilyn Fry, in the same book, notes that meanings "should arise from our bodily self-knowledge, bodily play, tactile communication, the ebb and flow of intense excitement, arousal, tension, release, comfort, discomfort, pain, and pleasure" but that the "vocabulary will arise among us . . . only if we talk with each other about what we're doing and why, and what it feels like."

Dr. SDiane Bogus writes, "I wish for the lesbian nation a consciousness of our sexuality for our strength lies in it. We gain inspiration by the loving that passes between us. And that inspiration is brought into being by the outstretched dyke hand." (*Dyke Hands & Sutras Erotic & Lyric*)

Magazines like *Quim* (For Dykes Of All Sexual Persuasions) and *On Our Backs* (Entertainment For the Adventurous Lesbian) present a street-wise entertainment package designed to be provocative and outrageous, and books like *Bushfire*, edited by Karen Barber, push behavioral and perceptual boundaries.

A plethora of sexual art and literature for women has been published since 1987. For Karen Barber lesbian sex writing is hip, hot and fun. Photographer Della Grace (*Quim*) produces work that is transgressive, deconstructing "our notions of Woman, of Lesbian and of Perversion in order to create a space for the exploration and celebration of diversity and desire."

The Sheba Collective note in their introduction to *More Serious Pleasure* that the stories they received for their second erotica volume had "sustained story lines and interesting plots" along with "straightforward sexual encounters and sexual fantasies."

Along with the current richness of words, images, and activities, however, it is important to remember Margaret Sloan-Hunter's caution that "the assumption that lesbians know it all leaves little room for growth." (*Yantras Of Womanlove*)

Like Susan Hawthorne and Jenny Pausacker in *Moments of Desire*, I've noticed that "there is no consensus...that one word is too crude or that another is a euphemism. Women are still making exploratory choices about language: when to name and when to indicate, when to use colloquial terms and when to use image and metaphor." Each book which is published is a victory over silence, each story charts and preserves a little more territory.

Still, for me, there is infinite room for more. No book is or can be definitive. What we need is a discourse, a language which is evolving, playful, detailed, encompassing, terrifying, transcendent. In the oh-so-hip 1990s, it may be useful to remember that we come to our sensual awareness slowly and move from deep within our bodies outward. In most of the U.S. and the world lesbian sexuality is still censored and often illegal. Writing erotica is a radical and extremely political act.

Afterglow, More Stories Of Lesbian Desire, edited by Karen Barber, Alyson, Boston.

An Intimate Wilderness: Lesbian Writers On Sexuality, Edited by Judith Barrington, The Eighth Mountain Press, Portland OR.

Bushfire: Stories Of Lesbian Desire, edited by Karen Barber, Lace, Boston.

By Work Of Mouth: Lesbians Write the Erotic, edited by Lee Fleming, Gynergy Books, Charlottetown, Prince Edward Island.

Dyke Hands & Sutras Erotic & Lyric, poems and essays by SDiane Bogus, WIM Publications, San Francisco.

In Her I Am, by Chrystos, Press Gang, Vancouver.

Lesbians Ignited, poetry by Carolyn Gammon, Gynergy, Charlottetown, Prince Edward Island.

The Lesbian Sex Book, by Wendy Caster, Alyson, Boston.

Moments Of Desire: Sex And Sensuality by Australian Feminist Writers edited by Susan Hawthorne and Jenny Pausacker, Penguin, NY.

More Serious Pleasure: Lesbian Erotic Stories & Poetry, edited by the Sheba Collective, Sheba Feminist Publishers, London.

On Our Backs (periodical), edited by Marcy Sheiner, Blush Entertainment Corp, San Francisco.

Quicksand: African American Lesbian Erotica, poetry by Folisade, BAP, Palo Alto, Ca.

Quim (periodical), edited by Lulu Belliveau and Sophie Moorcock, London.

Serious Pleasure: Lesbian Erotic Stories & Poetry, edited by the Sheba Collective, Sheba Feminist Publishers, London.

Somebody Should Kiss You, poetry by Brenda Brooks, Gynergy, Charlottetown, Prince Edward Island.

Sous la Langue/Under Tongue, by Nicole Brossard, Gynergy, Charlottetown, Prince Edward Island.

Tidelines, edited by Lee Fleming, Gynergy, Charlottetown, Prince Edward Island.

Wanting Women, An Anthology of Erotic Lesbian Poetry, edited by Jan Hardy, Sidewalk Revolution Press, Pittsburgh, Pa.

Yantras of Womanlove, Tee Corinne, Jacqueline Lapidus, and Margaret Sloan-Hunter, Naiad Press, Tallahassee FL.

Seven Days in August

Paula Neves

I thought Luisa had a distinctly American habit. I don't know why; I'm sure it's a common reflex for most people anywhere to glide their thumbs across the rim of a glass or mug after having drunk wine or coffee or whatever, to wipe off lipstick or just the press of bodily evidence. I watched her do it now, her thumb stroking lazily back and forth across the top of her teacup, wiping it all clean. I don't know why I considered it an American characteristic; maybe I wanted to take her out of context, or at least put her where I thought she belonged. Strong rays of midmorning sun came in through the kitchen window. I let the heat soak into my back and shoulders, wishing I could take my shirt off to feel it better.

"What are you thinking about?" she asked, interrupting her own story about who'd been showing up at the dances and parties for this summer's *noitadas*. I had hardly recognized any of the names, but then I hadn't been paying much attention.

"Did you pick that up when you were in the States?" I asked, indicating the cup.

"What?" she asked.

"That – that cleaning off the lipstick you do with your thumb. On the cup." The sudden burst of words had been very awkward, I knew. But she smiled. The last traces of her lipstick made her full lips even fuller, or maybe that was just my impression from sitting as close as I was. In a family of mostly thin-lipped people, she had always stood out – the older cousin I looked up to, though we were both now at ages where four years didn't matter so much, or so I liked to think. Besides, she had always been the one asking me about music, rifling through the new cassettes I brought over every summer, asking if the videos that played here on the government channels were the same as the ones playing at home. We always exhausted several afternoons and evenings just catching up.

"You're getting better," she said, raising her eyes, obviously referring to my Portuguese. It had been many years since I'd had the luxury of being around those eyes long enough to figure out just what shade of green they were, remembering only that they darkened depending on her mood. It had also been many years since I'd heard my parent's language spoken so fluently. One month a year of practicing after eleven months of disuse was not enough, but it was better than nothing.

"You'll just have to teach me some more," I said, then added quickly, "So that I won't forget, I mean. And can take something back."

But she knew what I had meant the first time.

"*Certamente,*" she said.

It was noontime. Her parents and brother would be coming in from the fields soon. I got up to go.

"Will I see you later?" I asked, in English.

"Of course," she replied.

From my first summer visit after she'd left we had been meeting in the evenings while her family – all distantly related to me somehow (I doubted there was any real blood left, but we all called each other "cousin" – practically everyone in the village called each other "cousin" or *tio/tia*), and mine were at the cafe taking their after-dinner espressos, *bicas*, and beers. When she came by, we sat in the cool darkness of my grandfather's orchard, watching as the stars gradually stood out sharp and silvery against the black velvet sky. We sat against the trunk of the medlar tree that grew by accident in the middle of the neat rows of pears or climbed it and sat as high up as we could without being seen.

Tonight, we sat in her family's arbor, inhaling the cool musky scent of the August evening. Every now and then a brisk breeze brushed the leaves and the rows of overripe corn in the field before us.

"You're cold," I said, noticing the gooseflesh on her arms

and her nipples pressing almost painfully against the thin cotton of her jersey.

"No, I'm fine," she said, shuffling closer to me on the bench. "O-K?" she asked, the exaggerated accent taking the edge off and allowing me a nervous laugh. I didn't exactly know why I was nervous, except that maybe we had run out of 'catchin up' to do.

"You know, Luisa," I started, "We spend so much time together, but sometimes I feel like – I don't know. . ." Why I had started on that line, I didn't know. The answers to my questions were as obvious as my being there, but at the time, I simply needed to say something to distract myself. Feeling foolish, I drank down some of the red wine she'd poured for us. It tasted unbearably bitter in that way that homemade brew usually is.

"Of course you don't know," she stated, "Not anymore. We see each other a few weeks a year, exchange a couple of notes the rest of the time. What do you expect?" She had turned away from me and was gazing out at the line of crumbling cottages that marked the end of the field.

"I don't know. Why does it have to be this way?" I asked, suddenly feeling disappointed that she was so matter-of-fact about it all, while I strained to catch every word, always hoping there was more feeling there than there was; she did not seem at all fazed that she'd been brought back here against her will, that we only saw each other now a few weeks a year.

She told me why, recounting facts I knew by heart without the slightest self-consciousness. As she talked, her shoulder alternately pressed and brushed against mine, giving the action the friction and warmth of bare skin rubbing against bare skin. I would have been happy just to peel back the sleeves of our shirts if I could have. It would have been enough.

"I still wish things were different," I said again, emboldened by the wine, but perfectly fluent.

"So do I," she said. She looked at me a moment, her expression softening, then abruptly got up – the wheels of her family's pickup were crunching up the drive.

The next morning, my mother wanted to go to Curia to take

the waters and maybe do a little shopping. She asked me if I wanted to go along. I agreed, feeling the need to be away from the village for a while, to relieve the heaviness that felt like a concrete slab pressing down on my chest.

On the well-kept, slightly shabby grounds outside Curia's spa, people, mostly middle-aged and elderly, moved about in a faded paean to gentility. Farmers, country gentlemen for the day, wore their straw boaters and good summer suits, shirts and coats open to the breeze blowing off the lake; their wives wore their best patterned dresses and faux pearls, shoes and bags matching. In my torn cut-offs, white t-shirt and sandals, I stood out, to say the least. Mother hassled me about it briefly: "Can't you ever wear anything appropriate?" But she was glad enough for the company to quiet down. She used to come here all the time with her own mother. They had both been great believers in the medicinal properties of the waters, though no amount of the precious liquid could've prevented my grandmother's stroke 14 months before. Still, as we neared the hall with the public fountain, my mother, as if on cue, sighed, "If only your grandmother had taken more treatments here last year . . ."

Inside, regulars and hotel guests sat looking mummified against the marble walls. Laid out on ancient wicker chaises, most were asleep behind their sunglasses and linens.

Down at the fountain, white-garbed, expressionless women dutifully took clients' measured bottles and glasses, filled them with gray-looking water, and handed them back over the railing where the hordes leaned anxiously. My mother had her own oblong glass from previous years. Visitors drank water from common glasses that the attendants cleaned by rinsing briefly under the continuously running spigots. I didn't think this was such a good idea, hygienically, but as a particularly dour attendant took away her clean glass, my mother elbowed me in the ribs and urged, "Drink, drink. It's good for you." Against my better judgement, I reached down to take another glass and quickly drank the sickeningly sulphurous stuff before I could think about the feel of my lips on the smeary edges of the glass. It was nothing like drinking from a lipstick-smeared cup.

"Luisa, what are you doing here?" my mother asked, and I would've gladly spit out the damn water in surprise if it had been any real surprise at all. Bewildered, I looked up in the direction of my mother's voice, but Luisa was already there, in a pale yellow summer dress, her thighs outlined against the fabric, the angle of light coming from the high windows hinting that she was not wearing a slip. I registered all these details, feeling heat prickling on the back of my neck, before I realized how annoyed, almost angry I was that I could not even get away for a morning. Get away and be an anonymous tourist for a little while. A tourist who would say goodbye again too soon.

"*Ola Tia* Helena. Hello Margaret," she greeted both of us but her eyes stayed on me. She smiled. She was wearing lipstick again.

"Hi." I mumbled.

"It was such a beautiful morning. I finished all my work at the house. Antonio didn't go into the *praça* today, so I borrowed his truck." At least that explained her being there.

Red lipstick, yellow dress, and a dusty truck, I thought, picturing it with some amusement.

"And why not," my mother encouraged. "You must get bored sometimes in that house."

"Well, not all the time. Margaret comes over and keeps me company." She glanced at me and I felt myself stiffen slightly.

My mother liked Luisa, always had. Luisa was feminine, always dressed appropriately, and my mother never failed to notice. "That's a pretty dress," she remarked, true to form. "I wish Margaret here would take a lesson or two from you."

"Well, I'll try to teach her." This time Luisa winked at me and, uncomfortable though I was with her risky nonchalance, I still couldn't resist the playfulness of it. Luckily, my mother was beyond it all.

"Isn't it wonderful that here you can relax any morning of the week?" My mother gushed. I heard the familiar strains of nationalistic sentiment coming on. "Yes, you don't find many places like this in the States," I mimicked, finishing for her.

"Don't be impertinent," she chided, poking me lightly in the arm. "Luisa doesn't regret coming over, do you honey?"

"Well, it was really my family's decision to come back." It was a neutral enough answer, but I liked the courage it showed in implying it had not been her choice.

Mother eventually went off to her waters again, leaving us to stroll the walkways around the lake, and take the requisite tour of the Hotel Palace garden. Because we were both women and could get away with it, Luisa slipped her arm through mine as we walked. I was not that annoyed anymore. I did not even ask her why she had followed me here today.

"Tomorrow, I'd like to take you somewhere. After lunch, when everyone's down for a *sesta*."

"Yes," I replied, "I'd like that."

"I already know where you're taking me," I said when she came by the house the next afternoon. "Well then, let's not waste time getting there. Hop on." We risked getting killed riding on one bike, especially on these crazy twisting roads, but I saw the wisdom of doing it this way. One bike, evidence of only one. She was wearing shorts and a tank top and I concentrated very hard on not running my hands up and down and around to the front of the ribbed material. But I did hold on tightly to her like I had when we were kids winding wildly in tandem through the streets of Newark, her always in the front, guiding me on some adventure. She pedalled quickly, the smooth strong muscles of her thighs fluidly contracting. The quiet fields and tracts of sweet-smelling eucalyptus and pine seemed to fly by, though I'm sure we couldn't have been going very fast.

Finally, some distance off the main paved road, we pulled onto a narrow dusty one cut through a badly tended vineyard. It was impossible to ride any further, so we got off the bicycle and walked it down. She walked in front of me, her shoulders and arms damp from the exertion of the ride. She did not look back at me or speak to me. I had no idea how far she was going to take me, and I admit I was a little apprehensive, but I didn't say a word either. After all, I had wanted this long enough, hadn't I? Some wild black raspberries grew along the sides of the swath, tangling with the vines and contrasting with the vivid green of the grapes. *Those* were the color of her eyes, I realized, having had it everywhere in front of me the whole time. Abruptly, she stopped and pushed the bike into a thick patch of vines. Taking my hand, she pulled me down one of the rows. It opened onto a small clearing.

"Here," she said, turning to me. She slid her arms around me, guiding her hands so that they slowly felt every inch from my waist to my back around to my breasts. I could not breathe, it was too much at once. Too much after too long without. "Wait," I said.

"I can't wait. You have only a week left. I can't wait again."

"No, that's not what I mean. I mean I – can't stand up –"

"Shh, it's ok, I understand," she said, pulling me down onto the ground.

"Our clothes," I remembered, "They're going to get dirty –"

"Maybe," she said, the last thing she said before my cut-offs, t-shirt and underwear were off and tossed up on some vines. She held me kneeling against her as her mouth found my neck, traveling down to bite lightly along my collarbone, leaving lipstick smeared on the way down. Her free hand pushed my damp thighs apart and plunged in with the voracity and knowing of someone who'd practiced this many times in her mind. Someone like me, who'd thought about this moment so long I should've known just what to do as well, but couldn't; she was having me, taking me first, and I let her. I let her lead me down the crowded streets of familiar neighborhoods, past lush country vistas to this place where only one language was spoken and understood. Her fingers fanned out inside me, closed, and pushed against the last resistance until I was on the verge of blacking out from pain and wanting. I tried to hold her arms down to slow her, to draw it out, but she deftly lowered me onto my back and spread my legs as far apart as they would go.

"Tell me, I always wondered how you'd want me to fuck you," she whispered, but I don't know if she really said it, if I thought it, or if I had wanted her to say it. It didn't matter. My nails dug convulsively into the loamy ground as she thrust with both tongue and fingers, savoring all of it in the eternal present, forever now. I began to buckle long before I was ready to, and when I started to fall back, still hearing our breathing far away, feeling her full weight slowly bear down on me, I came to and looked up into eyes that were as dark as the earth we were laying on.

"We don't have much time, do we?" I asked, when I recovered.

"Don't worry." she said, smiling down at me. "They're all still sleeping it off from lunch. Besides, nobody comes out here." She lowered her mouth again, but this time I stopped her.

"If you won't worry, I won't worry," I said, holding her face, making her look at me.

For an answer, she rose up until she sat straddling me. Raising her arms, she slowly peeled her shirt off. She had not worn anything under it – I hadn't even noticed. Her breasts hung heavy, the dusky nipples hard and sweetly vulnerable in the open air and light. Before I could agonize over it she said, "We have seven days, my love. Seven days and one long afternoon," and guided my hands up to her.

De Vilde Chayes – The Wild Beasts

Jyl Lynn Felman

This is about the erotic. My erotic. About when you see me my erotic. And when you don't. This is about the erotic. My white non-white ethnic white erotic self. About when I'm seen and when I'm not. Seen at all. This is about my erotic. And my sisters erotic. Our *sephardic ashkenazic mizrachic* erotic. And what you see. When you think you are seeing our *sephardic ashknazic mizrachic* white non-white ethnic white erotic selves. And what you don't see. When you think you are seeing me. If you are seeing me. At all. Are you seeing a luscious wild *vilde chaye* a *zaftig svelt kayn aynhoreh* stunning *vilde chaye?* Or are you seeing loud pushy money lender big nose zionist oppressor that you want to fuck? In the ass. This is about the erotic. My erotic. My white non-white ethnic white erotic self. About when I'm seen as white and when I'm not.

I stand before you exposed in my erotic. Are you seeing hot and wild? Or are you seeing nature's original biblical exotic? Standing in Eve's garden. With the apple of desire poison in my hand. Tell me. I want to know. What point in your desire I become The Forbidden strange exotic who steps right off your Christian page. Then comes too close to your open legs with my open mouth that always wants too much can't get enough. And is never full. This is about the erotic. My erotic. About when I'm seen as white and when I'm not. This is about the pleasure and the pain. Your pleasure is my pain. Your desire is my shame. My olive *sephardic* white *ashkenazic* colored *mizrachic* shame. In your fantasy and on my back I am the *hazar* your mother warned you about. The dirty smelly round thick piece of *treif* that you love to lick suck and chew in your fantasy but never really see. Me. In my full erotic self.

This is about the nazi that you get to be (come). In your fantasy and on my back. I saw you yesterday. I did. Walking down the street in your tall black leather boots. Striding straight ahead. Moustache lovingly placed above your lip. Disguised to all but me who dared to really look and see your blonde hair parted down the right and greased directly back. While your blue eyes pierced the night. This is about the nazi that you get to be. Disguised to all but me who dared to see the outline of your breasts pressed flat against your chest and hidden tight beneath a very fitted vest. What did you think that I would think at the heavy sound of your knee high kicking boots. That this is consensual? As you bend your gender to expand the narrow rules of what we all can be. What do I become? What do I become as you expand the rules to fit your fantasy? This is about the erotic. My erotic. My white *ashkenazi* olive *sephardic* colored *mizrachi* erotic self. And how your pleasure becomes my terror. And my sisters terror. Haunting us with memories of the dead. Naked and shaved. Starved to the bone. I see you reach to touch your moustache with a flourishing of your female male female wrist. And I see the genitals of my relatives hanging limp. I hear the sound of your belt on my flesh. And now I am the blood libel the christ killer the dirty lascivous promiscuous defiler of your people. This is about the erotic. My erotic. About when I'm seen as white and when I'm not.

When I'm seen my erotic and when I'm not. Depends. On who I'm with and where we are. Are we public or are we private? Is this personal or political? When I'm finally seen in my erotic it is about the viewer's needs and not my own. From your eyes and not my own. When you need to feel politically correct and when you don't. I am the new prophylactic. Safe at either end. On the floor behind the couch in my living room. You begin to lick and whisper in my ear. Tell me. Tell me 'bout your people you whisper as you lick. I really want to know. You suck hard. When in erotic disbelief. I hear you tell me that my white non-white ethnic white but always European ass is actually politically correct. Tonight. And not considered sleeping with the enemy because after all is said and done my ass is a finely tuned historically positioned cultured ass. And that's okay. Tonight. It's got tradition that 'ol ass of mine. That white non white ethnic cultured ass of mine.

At the other end. Of this prophylactic stretch that we share. Someone else is talking to my ass. Again. This is what I hear. On my back. And in my ear. You're okay. She says barely holding hot desire in. I can sleep with you after all. She says. And be myself. I can even take you home to meet my mother. She's laughing in relief. In her cute erotic way. She's laughing with relief. Because she thinks she can truly take me home. She turns me over reaching with her hand. Before I open wet and wide I hear a singular erotic sigh. Filled deep with her relief. You're really white pink like me. Pink she says again as she takes another bite. No I scream. No. My erotic misbaving before my very eyes. I tell you. When I'm seen my erotic and when I'm not. Depends. On who I'm with and who I'm not.

Passionate **they** always say. A real *vilde chaye* our bodies in heat and hot pursuit A real *vilde chaye* my sisters alone we say to each other. You girls are so passionate. A *vilde chaye* I whisper. She smiles at me hungry for a piece of my erotic without knowing who I am. Hungry for more without knowing. Who I am. Or where I'm from. Her last lover couldn't take it but she knows I can. She tells me. We my white *ashkenazi* olive *sephardic* colored *mizrachi* sisters We are oh so passionate. And so verbally articulate. That we can take it. We speak fire and are safe at either end. The new prophylactic. *De Vilde Chayes* the wild beasts who spew fire with our bodies but are never seen. Never seen. At either end. But we know the erotic ethnic truth. The erotic ethnic truth that *De Vilde Chayes* are neither the gefilte fish nor chopped liver that you love to eat. No. *De Vilde Chayes* are another type of fetish. From the candy store. On the middle shelf. Individually wrapped. The exotic white non-white ethnic kosher type you might say. Safe. Within everybody's reach. On the middle shelf. Where we've always been. Anybody can eat us without really tasting who we are. But we know the erotic ethnic truth. We are another type of fetish. The exotic white nonwhite ethnic kosher type you might say. Anybody can eat a *vilde chaye* without tasting who she is.

In the end I'd like to speak about desire Yours for me and mine for you. How we want each other. From that burning roaring place inside the center of your belly and in mine. Inside the center of your belly and in mine. It is desire where I feel the wet heat rising hot from your flesh to mine. From my flesh to yours. Your tongue in me my tongue in you. Our mouths open wanting. This is about our wanting. In the end I'd like to speak about desire. Yours for me. Mine for you. Hot and hard across the culture line. Usually in private. But in the public's eye and on the many pages. Where are all the images? On the pages in the books. Where are all the images of my erotic *sephardic ashkenazic* and *mizrachic* sisters? We are absent from the stories. So that desire in the end is white or black. And we are never seen. My middle *zaftig* sisters and myself. Are never seen. Sometimes I wonder was my mother right? Is it better just to be a *knaydala* floating in the chicken soup week after week a dumpling floating in the soup. But then I swallow tasting my sweet lust me for you you for me lust to burning bursting lust Or was my mother right to be a *boobala* a nice Jewish girl rather than a *vilde chaye*? A wild raging *svelt* stunning *kayne aynhoreh vild chaye*. Sometimes late at night lying in my bed awake without the lights I wonder was she right. Is it better not to be. Ever seen. This is about the erotic. My erotic. My white non-white ethnic white erotic self. About what you see when you see me and when you don't. See me in my full erotic self.

GLOSSARY

Hebrew: the spoken and spiritual language of the Jewish people and the language that the Five books of Moses/the Torah is written in

Ladino: combination of Spanish and Hebrew; the language of the Sephardic Jews

Yiddish: combination of Hebrew and German; the language spoken by Ashkenazi Jews while Hebrew was reserved for study and prayer

Ashkenazim: Eastern European Jews from the former Soviet Union, Germany, Poland, Hungary etc.

Sephardim: Spanish Jews

Mizrachim: Middle Eastern Jews, from Iran, Iraq, Morocco and North Africa

De Vilde Chayes: Yiddish, wild beasts, our mothers warned us not be . . .

Zaftig: Yiddish, juicy, a plum, plumb buxom, a well-rounded woman, a compliment

Svelt: Yiddish, a physically full woman, a compliment

Kayn aynhoreh: Yiddish, a cultural expression that literally means the evil eye, but used in reverse as a compliment

Hazar: Yiddish, pig, dirty

Treif: Yiddish, Hebrew, food that is not kosher and ritually not blessed; food that is forbidden according to Jewish law such as pig and shell fish

Kosher: Yiddish, Hebrew, food that is ritually blessed and prepared; food that is permissable according to Jewish law

Knaydala: Yiddish, a dumpling, usually stuffed with chopped meat, a round, chubby woman (compliment)

Boobala: Yiddish, nice girl, innocent, sweet

The Coloring Book

doris davenport

I like pussies. Everyone knows all about that. Or, they think they do. People smirk and whisper and say rude things to me because they think they know. Once, a womon yelled, "Hey, freak – you can look at mine! For a million dollars." (Now, really. Just to look at? Even the grand canyon is free.) Anyway, it was not, and is not, like that, and I want to tell about how all this got started. It started with that coloring book.

Some of you know *exactly* what book I mean because you bought it by the dozens, and by boxes. *The Cunt Coloring Book* later called *Labiaflowers*. Personally, though nobody asked me, I liked the first title better. If anybody had asked me (and this is probably why they didn't), I would have called the book "Pussy to Color" or maybe "The Book of Pussies" but something with the word pussy in it. I like that word. That's what this is about. I like pussies.

All this started back in 1978, in Los Angeles, which is where I was at the time, but things like this just naturally start in LA or maybe San Francisco. Anyway, I'd heard about the book, and went eagerly to the Wymin's Bookstore. Found the book in the store and between the time when I reached my hand out and almost touched it, I got stopped.

"Can I help you?" she snapped, through no lips, in a doughy pastey-flat face, with steely cold blue eyes.

"Well, I want to look around a minute," I said, quite pleasantly, considering. Considering that I had a reputation for going off on entities like her. Considering that I was a regular customer in that store. They had a reputation for being like *that* but also, they kept the latest wimmin's books stocked and since I am a writer and an Addict to Reading, I went there often. Yes, I am an African-american womon, but by then, I should have been quite familiar to this gringa clerk. As I admirably controlled my annoyance and 400 year old attitude, it continued:

"Well, let me know when you're ready, and it might be a good idea to leave your backpack at the front counter," she simpered.

"Well, no. That is not a good idea. But you're welcome to stripsearch the bag as I leave," I said, imitating her nasal-drip voice. She flinched but went away since other customers had showed up at the desk. *Child!* The things I have suffered for Art!

If I'd been really in tune or paying attention to the Signs or the Spirits that day, I would have known that this little altercation was prophetic of the kind of disapproval and general *dissin* that I'd get, for trying to touch this particular form of art! And at that, I got it from all kinds of wimmin, from richly colored back to non-colored; all groups and nationalities and ages and abilities *and* classes and castes in between!

Anyway, I finally picked up the book, already liking the cover, and opened it, and got, well, embarrassed, and hot all over. Quickly checked to see if I was being watched. I was flussed all over. Disgusting. Not the book! But the way this sick world has made us so screwy and secretive about something as pretty and natural as pussy. So, there I was, huddled over this book, just like those perverts in raincoats in porno shops, when actually, I knew I was fondling a major Art Form of the Twentieth Century. Frantically, I checked the price, and my pocketbook; paid for my copy and got out of there (oh, I offered my backpack to Sis Chickenlips, but she was too shamed to check it) and got home just as fast as one of those old yellow buses would take me. Really had to struggle *not* to look at the book on the bus. I knew better than *that*.

Home, finally! Sat down in the middle of the floor with the book, and proceeded to ooh and ah, and grin and smile and just plain ole have a *good* time! Maybe I did drool a little, but not on the book. (I am always very careful of my art. Ask anybody.) Kept looking at the price, because it seemed to me the book should cost a lot more, like those big glossy books of Asungi, Georgia O'Keefe, Van Gogh. All I know is, it was early Friday afternoon when I sat down, and it was deep dark when I looked up again.

Except for my right hand, and my neck and head, I hadn't moved for hours. When I did get up, you know what I did? Wrong. (See how you are.) I got a glass of water, and my crayons. (Because I always keep art supplies with me, just in case.) Then, the hard part: which one to color first? And did I want "realism," "surrealism," "futurism," or just plain ole sweet and nasty? Hours later, I decided and chose one. Or two. Slowly and meticulously selected the colors, testing them first to make sure they were just right. When I looked up again, it was morning and I was not a bit tired. I felt refreshed and rested, like I'd been meditating in a Goddess Temple or something like that. In fact, I was energized, and besides, I had things to do.

Beating the trash collectors and neighbors to it, I found a nice wooden crate to use for a coffee table. Lots of my friends bought these huge, expensive, full color art books, and proudly (arrogantly and insolently, I thought) displayed them on coffee tables. One girlfriend had a copy of African batik patterns displayed just so. She kept it dusted, too, and *nobody* put coffee near that table. You could see why. So, I got my crate, and then, placed the coloring book at the perfect angle on top of it. And I sighed a deep contented sigh, like God did when she looked out and said, "That's good." Then, I went on with dinner preparations for Thelma and Chris. One of my favorite couples and two of my favorite people .

Thelma and Chris were coming over later that Saturday evening, on their fifth or fifteenth honeymoon. They had a long on and off again history, with some *heavy* shit between and behind then, but right then, they were on and they tickled me. When they were "off," I saw or heard from them individually. One would call or visit, and though they avoided each other, they always talked about the other, to me. In those phases, I rested my vocal chords. All I ever said was "Uh huh. Yeah. Yeah? *Yeah!*" and similar profundities. I liked them. Separate or together, I liked both of them, mainly because they were a little crazy and they both had a wild sense of humor. When they were in an "on" phase, their love could come down on 'em anywhere and anytime. That being the case, I'd told them that they could spend the night at my house, or borrow my bed, whenever they needed to. They blushed when I said that, looking coy and virginal like Lesbian Harlequin heroines. They cracked me up. Anyway, they came by that Saturday night.

"Hey, hey, *hey,*" they both said, as they came in the door, smiling, grinning and glowing.

"Looking *good,* one time!" I said, as we hugged and kissed. Chris had on one of her soft silk blouses, a bright red one, over tailored beige slacks. Thelma wore a black and gold sequined top, and black slacks. Chris was almost 6 feet tall and medium-built and she liked to drape her clothes over her frame. Thelma was about 5'4" tall, and round-voluptuous. (Too fat, to her. Just fine, to me.) They made a pretty couple, Chris' ivory and Thelma's chocolate colors. Both wore a little makeup, and both smelled real good. Made my eyes *and* nose happy. And I don't apologize for this: I love beauty and art, in all their manifestations, and that night, Thelma and Chris were a work of art!

We went through the rituals of how you doing and how you been with Rhiannon and "Alive!" singing "Step by Step" in the background. I adjusted the volume, double checked the Nina Simone albums stacked on the turntable, and lit another stick of musk incense on the altar. And, just like that, our party started! (I might as well add, here, that later, I was also accused of abusing "Alive!" and Nina, using them to further seduce wimmin, and that is also a lie. The fact is, I'd just *discovered* "Alive!" and played that one record non-stop, even when I was alone. Nina, along with Jimi Hendrix, were longstanding staples in my life.)

There we were, with music, wine, tequila, cigarettes, ashtrays, incense and each other, steady laughing and talking, as they sat down on the couch and saw *The Cunt Coloring Book.* They both shut up. Chris turned a deep, deep, red; Thelma went several shades browner, with a slight sheen. Thelma started to laugh, real loud, as her hand jerked toward the book. Picked it up – and *slammed* it back down on the table! Still laughing, like a fiend. Chris quietly said, "Let me see, too." She took it gently from

Thelma, hugging her at the same time. Chris opened the book, smiled all over herself, and lit up the whole apartment. So there they were. Chris, a candle, and Thelma, a brown sun. Both of them looked like they'd had some ultimate announcement of good news, even if they couldn't believe it. Then, they got fidgety and silly. Acted like no spot on my couch was comfortable as they kept scooting closer to each other, and to that book.

In less than five minutes, they got to the stage of "That one looks like you" ("you," they said, not "yours."). They guzzled the wine, though they rarely drank that much, and their cigarette smoke made the room look like an L.A. smog alert. They never stopped glowing. If anything, they got worse. So, I offered the crayons. What I do that for? They went through the same process I had, and then – being honeymooners – had to choose one to color together (steady squirming around on the couch), and had to pick *just* the right colors, and so on.

But I did leave out one thing, about what I did with the book before they came. I got a mirror and tried to look at *my* pussy, to match it up with one or two in the book. Just for the fun of it (none had a clit quite as big as mine, to tell the truth). Anyway, I watched Thelma and Chris get to the drooling let's-match-them-up stage, and since their colors and hair textures were different from each other, they really had fun!

"Dinner's ready," I said. They mumbled something about not being hungry or never being hungry – although, til that night, they really did enjoy my meals, especially Thelma. I was amazed. This book could ruin a dinner party! But as it turned out, Chris and Thelma *did* work up an appetite.

I went back in the kitchen and heard a sudden noise. When I looked, them two was gone, and I heard the door to my bedroom slam shut. Well. I stopped and laughed out loud at them, while they laughed from the bedroom. Most of the food went in the oven (baked chicken, fried fish, blackeyed peas and rice, macaroni & cheese and cornbread) and the salad in the fridge, and I stood there a minute. Stood there smiling, and thinking, I should at least write about the coloring book as sexual foreplay and *aphrodisiac.*

Meanwhile, giggles from the bedroom. (I noticed that in their hurry, they had knocked over my new coffee table, and taken the book *with them.*) Then, tense-quiet back there. It was about eight p.m. on a Saturday night in mid-summer. I lived in a fairly un-safe neighborhood, but as it was just barely dark, I decided to take a (very short) walk. To give them privacy, and also to get away from them. The fact is, I was *also* curious as to how their pussies matched up with the ones in the book!

Some few hours later, I knew. Ah – you want all those details too? You won't get them. When I came back, I was really kind of at a loss as to what to do with me, but first Chris, then Thelma called my name. They sounded like two little mischievous girls. They were breathless, expectantly waiting for the tone of my reply. (Because, anybody will tell you, I have strange and intense mood fluctuations. For all they knew I could just as easy have put them out.) I responded, "Yeeeeeees?" and I know they could feel and hear the smile in my voice, and the curiosity – as in, "what could you two possibly want with me?" To bring you some wine? Water? A towel? Food? All of which, eventually, I did bring them, or we brought each other. And yes – we compared pussies, ours with the coloring book, and each other's with each other's – and eventually, we did eat the food I'd cooked, and the next thing we knew, it was Monday morning. And the *next* thing I knew, I was being ex-communicated from the L-F community.

* * *

That movement – from the representation of the thing, to the thing itself. From art to nature. From the book to the bed. Ha ha ha. You *do* see what I mean, don't you? Sure you do. Or, you could if you wanted to. No, I do not claim that the coloring book had that affect on most of the wimmin who bought it. Maybe some of them sedately colored one or two cunts and put the book aside. Maybe some wimmin looked at that book, *without* wondering what the real pussies looked like. Unlike me. This is the main point, for now: I did not intentionally use that book to start a two day "threesome" with my two friends! Although I have a reputation for a lot of things, lechery is not – or was not – one of them. The coloring book, however, changed my representation, so to speak. Because of that book, I soon had a name as a pussy-hound and worse things.

So, okay, on one level, one lightweight and superficial level, there might have been the slightest bit of truth in that appellation, your honors. (Because I know it's a whole slew of you out there saying "But I know better." and "The hell you say." Just like I know there are quite a few out there with an unbelievably judgmental quirk to your otherwise fine minds. Hence the jargonistic tone, above. "Appellation," my ass.) That truth, I swear, is that I was overwhelmed with an insatiable curiosity and need to know *what lots of pussies looked like!* Before I got the book, I was, honestly, only curious about the one or two that I – well – came in contact with.

But after all, the cunt coloring book was just a sampler. An appetizer, if you will (or, whether you will or not, that's what it was). During the Chris-and-Thelma weekend, I seriously thought about a new career. Maybe I could be an assistant on the next volume of pussies – surely, there would be multi-volumes, from live models! Even Thelma and Chris got in on the speculations: we three could open a dyke clinic; a clit clinic; a "health farm" specializing in vaginal massages. And so on. Our partnership, alas, was doomed to remain speculative.

Honestly, the grapevine is how I got it first. That those two were having serious *public* fights, even at the Palms (and just what they were doing at that sleazy bar, I don't know) and it turns out, I was named as the responsible party: responsible for "alienation of affection," – by both partners! Can you believe that? All I was doing, was artistic, scientific investigation. What motive could be purer than that? Sure, I felt "affection" for both of them, but none of it was in the "lover" realm. They stopped speaking to me, yet kept talking to everybody else in the community, it seemed, but I didn't know that for a long time. By then, I had to move.

And too, there were these really unfriendly accusations.

That I used the coloring book as a substitute for a lover. That is a lie. Truth is, I was just recovering from an intensely satisfying love affair wherein we were both co-dependent enablers in being mutual perpetrators of varieties of emotional and psychological abuse, with amazingly addictive, miraculous sex! But, that is another story and right now, beside the point, except that *no* book could substitute for *that* womon, if you get my drift!

Anyhow, soon after that weekend, and before all this foolishness got started, I got a second copy of the coloring book. One for my visitors, and one just for me. One book stayed on my coffeetable, except for short excursions into my bedroom. No, it never got to the point where I was just picking wimmin up, *unlike some dykes I know* - who didn't even have the excuse of the coloring book. It was never like that. But if I met a likely womon, who seemed to have an open mind, well – I showed her the book. And it was a natural, organic, New Age step from that to "Show me yours and I'll show you mine." Wasn't it? You tell me you wouldn't have done that? Well, ain't you nice! What I have, though, even now – is an insatiable curiosity. Not, however, an indefatigable and battery-run tongue. My eyes could go on, forever, where the rest of me simply could not! Because of that, the weirdest things happened!

First, for only a few weeks – inspired by the coloring book – I seemed to be an impassioned, ever-imaginative lover. After all, one wanted to do homage to such pretty pussies, and to do it *right*. But after awhile, I just got real tired. All I really wanted to do, was to look. Well. Some wimmin just would not believe that, would not accept that, and would not keep their disappointment to themselves. They accused me of being a hypocritical tease and leading them on. One Sunday morning, I woke up to a silent, cold-blooded picket at my apartment. Signs saying "Exploiter of Wymin." "Eat yourself." "Go back to Georgia" and some other really, really ugly ones, too! Then, I had to move. Repeatedly. From Midtown to Silver Lake; from L.A. to other states in the USA, but it did no good. The scenario repeated itself. Every now and then, in spite of a few close friends who found this situation hilarious and not to be taken seriously, I would get real real pissed off. It's annoying, y'know, to move once a month.

Don't *you* think pussy is fascinating? And pussies are so different, so wonderfully wonderful and diverse. With so much personality! Plus, I'd got into a "study" of the more aged ones! Loved the ones with grey hairs, and lots and lots of wrinkles! (Not to mention those incredibly varied earthy, fruity scents and diverse textures of pubic hair.) That coloring book made me an expatriate.

Can you get to that???? *Not* my political convictions or beliefs (and I DO have those), not because I was dodging something real radical with a conservative end (like, jail); *not*, even because Europe is "more receptive to Black artists," although I have found that to be true, but because of that coloring book. And I would sue T.C., except – to tell you the truth – I just love that book so much, and love many of the things it's done for my life.

Like even now. Remembering the first time I saw that book, I get hot flashes and start twitching and squirming. Remembering this one succulent, sweet pussy that looked sort of like the one on page 15 (or 17). Makes my mouth water, now, some fifteen years later. And here in this farmhouse in Italy, a few miles outside Florence, I have made a promise to change my ways. (Also, I plan to stop smoking. They cost *way* too much, over here.) However, there *is* a lesbian community in Florence, and I'm sure they would love to see my vintage copy of *Labiaflowers*.

(Montespertoli, Italy June 5, 1992)

Sex Acts

Sandra Lambert

Scene 1.

Marta lays alongside Sarah rubbing her hand over Sarah's belly in wider and wider circles. Occasionally she brushes down into her pubic hair or smoothes her fingers over Sarah's nipples where they lay close to the rise of her belly. Sarah isn't sure if it feels good to have her nipples touched. She moves her arms closer to her breasts, maybe she'll cover them, but first she closes her eyes and feels the shape of Marta's hand running at that moment along the underside of her stomach, cupping it. It is a strong, wide hand with short fingers. Sarah recognizes its shape and says to herself, this is my lover's hand, no one else's, and notices how warm the palm is as it moves up her body. Sarah relaxes her arms, stretching them above her head as she arches her breasts up into Marta's hand and mouth.

The next time Marta's fingers reach across her pubic bone Sarah's cunt flares up. She wants Marta's fingers in her now, quick before her desire can switch off. She spreads her legs wide and lifts her pelvis. Marta lays a leg over Sarah's pulling it wider and keeps up her slow, steady touching. Sarah wonders why her lover won't do what she wants. She shakes her hips in desire and frustration. Marta keeps touching and then lays her large body over Sarah's. She props up on one elbow to keep her weight from being crushing and the other arm pins Sarah's hand above her head. Her mouth pushes against Sarah's neck and lips, pressing her head into the pillow. Sarah can see and touch nothing but Marta, her body blocks the light and surrounds her. Everywhere there is Marta. The mass of her pushes Sarah into the mattress, letting her feel the exact outline of her own body and know she is inside it. With her free hand Sarah reaches around Marta's neck pulling her down, encouraging her to distribute more weight on her body and at the same time she lifts up against the arm Marta has pinning her wrist. She likes how she can push hard and not move and how the pressure makes the edges of her skin solid. The steam rising from the small open spaces still left between them scents the room.

Marta is kissing Sarah and kissing her, mouth open, all over her face. The tightness in her jaw that Sarah seems to always carry with her threatens to make her gag. I can't, she thinks, I can't open my mouth wide. She opens it a little and Marta kisses her and runs her tongue just inside Sarah's lips. Then she mouths along the line of her chin up to her ear. Sarah closes her eyes and chooses to remember that she is in her lover's bed and it is her lover on top of her, and the smells all around are her and Marta's. Sarah recalls that her lover has told her that anytime she wants to stop she can, anytime. Marta is kissing back up to her mouth and Sarah doesn't open it any wider, but she feels the back of her throat relax and her lips soften.

Marta shifts a little to one side letting fresh air come between them. She releases Sarah's wrist and runs her hand down, lingering over the side of her breast and then circling along her thigh. Sarah opens her free leg wider, bending it way up at the knee. Once again Marta ignores her cunt and begins to squeeze Sarah's breast, alternating rubbing and pinching her nipple. She shifts some more and grabs hold of Sarah's other nipple with her mouth and sucks and Sarah can't believe how good it feels, how much she wants it, how hard she wants it. She pushes Marta's head against her breast wishing she would get it all in her mouth.

Sarah wants this to go on forever except that her cunt is laying open and her vagina needs something in it. She can feel the walls opening up. "The dildo," she whispers to the top of her lover's head and Marta reaches down between Sarah's legs and pushes her fingers up inside her. Sarah pushes back until knuckles press against her clit. Pulling away Marta gets out of bed and Sarah sees her lover look at her spread out, arms above her head with her legs bent up and open. Marta's body is so big that it seems to carry its own climate around with it, and the cool air chills Sarah as Marta moves away.

Sarah worries that she's made a mistake. She should have just kept Marta there doing what she was doing. She's risking all those feelings going away. Marta hums softly as she gets the dildo and the lubricant out of the drawer and comes back to the bed. She touches the inside of Sarah's thighs as she passes by and then prepares things, smiling to herself as she does. Sarah watches Marta rub her hands over the purple ribs, careful to get the jelly everywhere, and she remembers who Marta is and who she is. Marta lays back down along her side and runs the tip of the dildo up and down Sarah's cunt until she slips it in and then pushes. Sarah pulls back for a second until Marta grabs her nipple in her teeth, making her bear down. Suddenly Sarah wants it all, the dildo deep and fast, and Marta's mouth hard against her breast. She wishes Marta had more mouths and hands and then, soon, Sarah comes. Her orgasm brings with it that strange mixture of sexual joy and the relief of knowing she doesn't have to worry about sex for awhile. Then, as Marta wraps her body around Sarah's, the humidity between them pushes away all thought and Sarah, for the moment, relaxes into this new season of her life.

Scene 2.

Sarah knows she has to seduce Marta slow and easy. So she starts on Monday. They're discussing a coming up Thursday night date.

"The play starts at eight," Sarah says, "And no pressure or anything, but I'm going to do you beforehand. So get off work as early as you can." Marta giggles wildly. It's a deep, back in her throat, sort of grunting, very butch giggle, of course. As soon as she gets herself under control the protesting starts.

"No, no, no, sweetie. You'll be too tired. I take too long. It's not necessary. Really, let's just go to the play."

"Yes, it is so necessary. I'm your girlfriend and one of my girlfriend duties is to pay attention to your body, so on Thursday I'm making it a priority. I'll rest up in the afternoon and you get ready to spread those thighs." By this time Marta has reached the point of unabashed squealing.

During the rest of the week Sarah makes sure to keep reminding Marta of their sex date and what her plans are. On Tuesday Sarah picks Marta up from work.

"Oh, my feet." Marta groans as she gets in the car. "I spent all day at the sink washing beakers."

"Poor baby. But just hold out till Thursday. I plan to start with a nice foot massage." Marta looks confused for a moment or pretends to look confused. Sarah is never sure which it is.

Then she throws her hands up in the air and shakes them at Sarah saying, "The play, dear, the play. We're just going to a play."

Wednesday Marta is on the phone talking about her work. "That stupid Peter, he kept giving me these piddley things to do. But I was able to get all my supplies set up for tomorrow, which means I can load those gels first thing."

"How long does it take them to run," Sarah asks, pretending to be interested in Marta's work.

"Well, three hours. Then I have to let them cool awhile before refrigeration, but that's basically it."

"So it's a short day," Sarah comments innocently.

"Yeah, I should be done by four thirty at the latest . . ." Marta suddenly realizes Sarah's tone is a little too innocent and stops talking. Then she starts back up. "Uh, did I forget to mention. There's all this other stuff I have to do. You know how Peter is. Lots and lots of stuff. I'll be late, real late. I won't get out till just before the play. In fact, I think I'll need to meet you at the play. Oh well, it just can't be helped."

"Yeah, right," Sarah laughs. "I'll expect you around five."

"No sweetie, I can't. I'll be too sweaty after work, and we have to eat dinner first, and you already have a lot to do tomorrow." Sarah keeps laughing as Marta keeps on. "And I don't think tomorrow is a good day astrologically. I looked it up in the paper and these things are important, you know. We have to have our planets aligned."

"Don't worry about your planets," Sarah vamps. "I'll align them for you. See you at five."

After they hang up Sarah worries that maybe she's pressuring Marta too much and maybe she doesn't want to for real. So she calls back, and when Marta answers Sarah whispers into the phone.

"You know that you don't really have to do it, don't you?"

Marta drops her voice into a matching whisper and says, "Sure do." They hang up and Sarah goes to sleep thinking of Marta spread open in the sunlight.

By Thursday at six Sarah is getting anxious. She's trying to calculate the latest possible moment Marta can show up so that they still have time to have sex, when Marta walks in. She stands in the doorway of the bedroom and Sarah tries to figure out how to tell what Marta wants.

"Sorry I'm a little late," Marta says. "I went home to take a shower and change."

A shower, Sarah repeats to herself triumphantly. She took a shower. She wants it. Sarah knows everything is going to work out just fine.

"Why don't you come get on the bed?" Sarah asks. Marta moves into the room and Sarah turns around to arrange the pillows the way her lover likes them.

"This isn't such a good idea, you know. I think we should just go out to dinner. How about the new burger place?" Marta asks.

Sarah turns around thinking maybe Marta is serious, but there at the end of the bed Marta has taken off her vest and is pulling her shirt up over her head. As Sarah watches she kicks off her shoes and socks and slips down her pants. Still offering suggestions she climbs into bed with only her underwear left on.

"Or maybe sushi! If you insist we could eat Italian, but I just had pasta for lunch."

Sarah almost says something about "losing the underwear," but decides the way things are going she'll have it off soon enough. With just a little convincing Sarah gets Marta to lay diagonally on the bed, so that there is room for Sarah to sit at her feet. Sarah pulls out the oil she has stored beside the bed and begins to massage the foot propped up between her legs. Soon

Marta's chattering fades away and the room gets quiet. The evening light is softening all the colors with grey, and Sarah is glad she's turned off the phones and locked and closed the curtains on the front door. Marta has her arm thrown over her face. Sarah stops thinking about anything else but the foot she is rubbing. She feels how callused it is, and wide, and how there isn't much to the arch. She rubs at the edges of the heel and pushes her fingers into all the spaces and bones along the ankle.

Eventually, she pours out more oil and runs her hands along Marta's legs, moving herself up between them so she can reach higher. Curling her fingers above the waistband of the white cotton Jockey For Her undies, she pulls down.

Marta quickly tightens her thighs and pulls her arm off her face. She raises her head up and says, "Okay."

Sarah knows she means, okay that's enough, but demands, "Okay what?"

Marta looks at Sarah for a moment and then replies, "Okay, never mind," and drops her head back down on the pillow as she lifts her hips and Sarah pulls the pants the rest of the way off.

Wow, that was easy, Sarah marvels to herself as she starts rubbing along Marta's thighs slowly pushing them wider and wider. She replenishes the oil and slides her hand up and down the mounds of belly and breast and over nipples that are as hard and thick as bolts of steel.

Sarah pushes herself back a little so she can see between Marta's legs. There is a remnant of daylight left outside, but in that room, between Marta's thighs, under her belly, it is dark. Sarah lays her hand on top of Marta's pubic hair and pushes up, moving her cunt more to the surface, above the folds of thigh. With her other hand she spreads the lips and reaches in. She pauses a moment thinking Marta might lodge a protest, but nothing happens.

She's desperate now, Sarah thinks and decides to make Marta say it.

"Do you like this?" Sarah asks. "Does it feel good?"

Marta opens her eyes, looks at Sarah in the almost darkness, and smiles, knowing what Sarah wants.

"Yeah, it feels good," she replies and moves her hands over her own breasts as Sarah moves her fingers in and out down below.

"Do you think you'd let me lick you?" Sarah asks into the dark.

"Maybe," came the soft reply and Sarah repositions herself and pushes her face into Marta's cunt. They both know Sarah can't keep this up long enough for Marta to come, so Sarah explores and tongues, and pushes her jaw, and sucks along Marta's lips until her arms begin to ache too much. Then she lays her head against Marta's thigh and rests, playing her thumb over the clit in front of her. Soon she feels Marta's rhythm of tightening and releasing begin in her thighs and breath. The times of tension grow longer and longer as Marta builds herself up towards orgasm. Eventually Marta clenches her muscles and holds her breath for what seems an impossibly long time, finally releasing them in jagged spasms and silent gasps.

Sarah lets Marta wallow in it all for a little and then sits herself back up between Marta's thighs.

"So, this wasn't such a bad idea I had, huh?" she says with no small measure of satisfaction. "Yep, I planned this out well. You really wanted it, didn't you? The way you just spread those legs out wide." Sarah's satisfaction is quickly turning into outright smugness. "I do you good, don't I. In fact, at this moment, I feel like the Queen of the Femmes."

At that, Marta starts laughing and pulls Sarah down beside her, cutting off her monologue of self congratulation with a kiss to her still wet lips.

Scene 3.

Sarah and Marta have never been riding together before. Sarah uses her electric scooter instead of her wheelchair every chance she gets, but Marta hasn't been on her bicycle in years. She lives near the University, where the oppression of the young and slim has made being a fat dyke on a bike unsafe. But with the promise of quiet, secluded streets in a neighborhood of more regular people, Sarah has convinced Marta to bring her bike over.

After warning Sarah that she probably would only make it to the corner if, in fact, she remembered how to ride at all, Marta mounted her bike and took off. Sarah watched with delight as her lover made graceful circles in the quiet street, and then turned her dial to its fastest setting and scooted after her.

Now it's an hour later into their wanderings on a January afternoon, seventy degrees and sunny, and all around is that particular landscape of late winter in north central Florida. In the yards of small wood houses and concrete block duplexes camellia trees are losing their blossoms and some have perfectly round skirts of petals spread under them in all the shades of red. Tucked around them are often azaleas, the big purple ones usually, just beginning to show. It's been a mild winter so many houses have patches of tired out poinsettias leaning against them that were never quite killed by a frost.

Sarah has never ridden with anyone before and she's beginning to figure out that when she's in front she can't suddenly pull to a stop just because a pine tree is wrapped with trumpet vines, the thousands of orange flowers reaching thirty feet above her. And she can't swerve off to the left down a street that looks interesting when she's on Marta's right. At first this annoys Sarah, but as they get more skilled and figure out their own set of signals she begins to like it some. Especially when they curve fast around a corner together, staying close but never touching, like ice skaters or dolphins.

When they get back to Sarah's apartment she's tired and leaves Marta sitting outside to go take a nap. She falls asleep quickly waking up only once as Marta crawls in beside her. Curling into Marta's back, Sarah inhales the sweet, sharp smell of sun baked sweat laying between her lover's shoulder blades and drifts back into sleep.

That Second Wind

Coleen Carmen

Lena is touching me again. Her long, cool, freckled hands brush against my darker skin as she smiles, looking into my face. Laughing, she reaches to pull me in from the door, and lightly tucks her fingers around the soft inside of my arm. She narrates a story for us: something very ordinary with a twist. She doesn't falter over a word or detail or miss a stroke.

The chemistry between us is filling me; the game advancing. We are like gamblers, placing bets, but not yet ready to disclose our private lies or secret hopes. The pads of her fingers trace my arm in milky cat-kisses. "Ummm," I sigh to myself, and remember how my Grandmother played with my hair when I was little, lifting it over and behind my ears. How early I learned a certain touch from the right person could mean so much. Now, with Lena, something spectacular was happening. The heat in my groin magnifies.

Lena taps Gabe on the shoulder. He takes my jacket; she rushes to the kitchen. Gabe is smiling and squats on the edge of the bed. He seems nervous. Or is he amused? His eyelid twitches like a busy signal on a telephone – high pitch, then nothing.

I notice the big window just past him. The view, five stories high, faces southwest. Acres of flat, rolling streets flow out to the sea: endless rows of gray asphalt, that stretch like fingers, to sand, then ocean. the Sun's warmth seeps through the glass. I take it all in and soon find myself yawning with pleasure.

Was it only a week ago, or two, that Gabe and Lena came to my place, the three of us drinking sparkling cherry cider, toasting the approach of summer, and laughing while we picked Dolmas from our teeth? I wanted to do everything right. No use pushing the river. I needed clues *and* a little patience. Yet, I kept wondering which one of us was going to make this silly mess official?

Lena's touch makes me wet before my mind has a chance to vote. I want her alone – and soon.

A faint bubbling surfaces from the kitchen. In this delicious moment even the furniture listens. Scents sift into the room: buttery garlic, sweet red peppers, ham hocks, steaming black beans and cilantro. I'm being told just how much Lena has looked forward to cooking for me. Sunlight brushes against the building in teasing waves. Four O'clock Sunday never had it so good, I might have said aloud.

Gabe's feet are planted like sticks in mud. He hums a sparse tune and finishes rolling a 'cigarette.' He often reminds me of a well traveled sailor who has only recently found land again. His hair is hot and cool, blue-black like crows eyes and thinning in some places. His eyes meet mine in the slur of this golden light. He winks at me. This moment has the instantaneous bite of another place or time. Are we engaging in a form of archaic ritual where friends face as rivals? Like swimmers competing for the day's prize, we welcome the dangers of high water and for all our unspoken reasons, are content to ignore the shore.

Lena is shouting. She waves her hands at us as if scrubbing an invisible wall. Then she grins and, raising a eyebrow to Gabe, asks him if he has bothered to fetch me a drink. She leans over and her long, light brown hair sweeps my thigh. She kisses me on the cheek and tells me how it's not nice to keep a woman waiting.

Gabe motions for me to come to the table. He lifts my offering out of the freezer, uncorks the bottle, and pours three glasses. I think back of our days at the print shop. For over a year I brewed the daily pot of Graffeo coffee and dealt with the front counter. In exchange he bought the 'Half and Half' and printed my lesbian newsletters. We had the model 'work' relationship. We were friends. Then I met her . . .

The first time I heard Lena's deep, melodious voice, I could barely breathe. Something unexplainable and warm and unknown to me – previously untouched, suddenly *expanded* in her presence. I had kept my feelings contained until now. How long could I wait?.

Lena bends in front of me again; her cool skin close to mine, her scent covering me. I am wet with desire for her. My cunt is pulsing, singing the sacred first notes of hunger, of lust, and of love. What does she expect of me? What does she want? And Gabe? What is going through his mind?

Lena pouts her hips against the bread board and lifts the half-smoked cigarette to her lips. She opens her legs. My mouth fills and I know it's not the wine. No one said this was going to be easy.

"You're so solid and strong, Nessa. Thin, too. Round in the right places, unlike me."

Gabe listens as we compare our specific womanly grievances of which we've had no choice but to inherit: my height, her hair, her breasts, my breasts.

"C'mon, Nessa, tell me you don't ever workout. I would love to look even a little bit like you."

Lena looks youthful and radiant in her thread-bare blue cut-offs and open cotton shirt. I love the way she rolls up the sleeves not quite equally, exposing the softest skin I have ever felt. With her left hand she scoots her wine glass onto the kitchen table and turns to me. Her face is suddenly close. With tender precision Lena gingerly exhales one long fragrant wave of smoke into my forehead, then, as sure as the sun and the moon, she plants herself at my side, next to the shimmering edge of the window, as if she had been there all of her life.

Asleep, in dreams, or sometimes wide awake: Lena is *there*. Call them visits or visitations: they happen regularly and each one is the same. Before I am fully conscious she is on me, all over me, her freckled arms wrapped around us like bright birthday ribbon. She pulls me in by the waist and fits me to her. Her heart speaks now in its truest tones and we're teasing each other, like lovers do, noses pressing into cheeks.

I follow her into the bathroom. Lena brushes against the door which closes to a delighted click. When I clutch a few strands of hair into my hand a glide their cool, silky length across the back of her neck, she gasps and urgently leans her throat deliciously close to my mouth. Then, just north of the ear, where her hairline ends, I begin to kiss her ears, neck and shoulders. Her bra-strap rests on her biceps and the curve of her breast surrenders completely in our embrace. She is sighing in little gasps and I *knew* it would be like this. My heart bursts open, my cunt plump with happiness. She sings my name. Whispers "Nessa, give me what you've got. Don't stop."

My lips greet and teeth close slightly, coaxing her babyfinger onto the warm swollen hollow of my tongue. I kiss her hard, letting her finger escape slowly. I enter her mouth with my middle finger, still kissing her, though softly now, and lead her mouth to my breast, my fingertip firmly stroking the silky crevice behind her lower teeth. She sucks and teases my breasts; swims in my smell. I need her again. Quickly I kiss her mouth and pin her arms at her sides. Then, all over her belly and groin I trace for shadows of skin, hair or bone, and linger there with my tongue, hands, nose and cheeks. Her scent, like her voice, fills me and brings me home. I can't get enough. All around me is the clean metallic aroma of a rainstorm.

But I have not followed her into the bathroom. Lena lazily winks and fills my glass. I blink once; then again. A cold shiver strays from my heart.

Out the window one final burst of orange softens near the horizon. I stare at my hands, my watch, looking for a way to measure where the time has gone. Finding no answer, I put the glass down and move to the threshold of the door. There's no compass here. No experts to call. no map worth its paper, no mirror. Only my heart, proud and lost.

"What's the matter? Ness! Where are you going?"

How can I tell them? The words are already ruined and desolate: silvery moth wings crushed to powder. I pivot in the hallway and look back at my friends.

"I can't stay. Listen, I can't live this way. I won't do it. I'm sorry."

I want to say, "Call me in a month." Instead, I offer only the smallest grin and wave good-bye.

Immediately, I descend five flights of stairs, leaping then landing on what once must have been plush and fluffy carpet.

I could have followed her into the bathroom, or better yet, could have rascalled her over to my place. Damn Her! I could have taken her into my arms and, prompting her with the strength and voice of my heart, shown her how heat can move through limbs at will. A single kiss could have shown her how heat changes breathing into a melodic roar – like long awaited rain.

I feel my body swerve. If I were a different person, or maybe the kind of woman I used to be, I might have given myself away. Instead, I let the brass plated door of the lobby slam solidly behind me: the sound bending in sharp, sad, invisible angles. Slowly, I move on, knowing soon I will find a reason to put back the bounce in my step.

The Event

Shelley Rachor

The cold tile of the jail wall was a surprise to the wet sweat heat of my back. I lurched forward involuntarily from the shock. The drumming of my heart was like a thousand butterfly wings beating against my chest, but my heart was in my loins.

My chest expanded with each breath I could not take. My senses were heightened beyond anything I had imagined. I thought for a moment that I would surely die from the intensity of it all and *that* would be okay.

The combination of the salt sweat dripping into my eyes and the steam from the raining showers on either side of me added to the drama and filtered lens view. The stinging of the salt forced my eyes shut and caused me to breathe when I would have chosen not to.

When I was able to open my eyes just a little I was wonderfully assaulted with a view of a crystal river flowing between the mist shrouded hills of my eighteen year old upright breasts. I could feel the vibrations of sound and lips on the down of my belly and could see in the light cloud just above my eyes: "You have a beautiful body, baby." But I could not hear.

I was being powerfully, but gently driven back to the wall at my hips. My eyes followed the steaming river down the muscle valleys of my abdomen to where it overflowed my navel and spilled over my pubic hair like a rainbowed Niagara Falls. Resting elegantly on my hip bones and across my stomach were ten long and well-manicured arrows. A spreading fan of fingers, they began to inch upward.

The length of the fingers testified to the six foot two frame of the beautiful light-skinned mahogany woman folded so regally at my feet. Suddenly, two dark lashed golden curtains lifted and I was over the waterfall and into the sea-green almond eyes of the Amazon. I gasped in the air I so desperately needed and now was able to hear the bright ribbon of her chuckle.

The air was taken away again when the fingers encircled my waist and the oval nails dug crescent moons deep into the muscles of my back. I felt the searing salt again, but I could not tell if it felt like pleasure or it felt like pain. I had no frame of reference. One thing was certain, it *felt* exquisite.

My arms which had been resting spellbound against the wall began to move toward the shoulders of the goddess, but my arms were heavy and I was slow. The flight of her fingers was swift as she cupped my elbows and raised my arms straight above my head in one movement. In that same movement she unfolded to her knees and the dry heat of her mouth was parallel to by breast. She wrapped my fingers tightly around the shower faucets on either side of me above my head. "Don't let go 'til I tell you, baby."

The word "baby" was said wet as her tongue began swimming lazily in the salty river on my body. From her knees, she coiled and uncoiled herself like a dancing serpent while her tongue began swimming faster and left a wake like a water skier all over my flinching belly. Her head finally stopped under my chin while she let her tongue paddle around in the pool that had formed at the base of my neck. Delicately, she bit a necklace of kisses. Her nails were making feather trails over my breasts and dropping off my alarmed nipples to drip down my sides. I was being tenderly mauled by gossamer claws and this, too, was exquisite.

Her lips were smiling within an inch of my breast. My nipple was all attention and straining to reach her when her tongue nudged it back while half my breast was pulled into the oven cavern of her mouth. She released the pulsing peak with a well placed nipple nip and I yelped.

Her mouth was over mine in a flash, taking my valuable air and my cry. "No noise, baby. You'll get us busted. I'd like to play with you for hours, youngblood, but the Sarge will be back any second to lock us down. I'm going to take care of business now, baby. Hold your mud, girl."

Still on her knees, she lifted my legs easily over her shoulders and cradled my narrow hips in her hands. I felt the hot breeze of her breath ruffle through my pubic hair. The moment her mouth found its way between my legs, the flood gates of my woman's world were flung wide and wave after wave of warm wet spilled over her lips and onto my thighs. Every muscle in my body was dancing independently to the rhythm of her long, low chuckle.

From somewhere in the forest deep within me began the rumbling of a great roar that gathered voice as it traveled its way to my vocal chords. Just as my voice escaped and began to crack the steam clouds surrounding us, her mouth once again covered mine. She was standing now, and as her tongue danced with mine in the eye of the roar, her fingers danced their way into the volcanic opening to the world of me. As she discovered the hidden passages to my pleasure. so did I. Four fingers penetrated deep, without a scratch, and the chalice of her palm was the cup I runneth over.

It lasted some moments, this acute awareness. Still clinging to the shower faucets as I had been told, my body fell lifeless, (or life-full?) against the tile. I was soaked from head to toe, inside and out, and not from the still raining showers.

"Let go the faucet, baby. Shit. Let go, fool! We gotta' get outa' here **NOW!**"

With effort, she pried my fingers loose and I slid, less than gracefully, down the wall to land in a soggy heap at her feet.

"Shit. I don't have time to fool with you, girl. Come here."

She scooped me up in her arms like a crane and in a few long Serenghetti strides we were out of the shower. As she dumped me unceremoniously on one of the six cots in the cell we were met by applause and laughing cheers from our cellmates. She hovered over me long enough to whisper, "I brought you out, baby. You remember that and pass it on."

She took her chuckle and quickly leapt into her own cot as we heard the approaching tambourine clanging of the sarge's keys. If I could have found my voice I would have said thank you.

The Prom Queen

Chea Villanueva

Toy and Rocky were going to the prom!

Toy wore a green chiffon dress over top of a black slip, black bra, garters and stockings. Her teased hair was held together with Aquanet Hair Spray and My Sin Perfume.

Rocky, on the other hand, wore a baby blue tuxedo, ruffled shirt with topaz cufflinks, and hair slicked back with Olivo, smelling like an AquaVelva commercial. Rocky had spent all day pomading her black hair to a gloss, while Toy spent all afternoon padding her bra to a 36-C.

After the prom they planned to make out in Rocky's blue 66 Malibu. They had been doing this every night for a year, but tonight would be special because of the prom.

Toy and Rocky walked in, hand in hand. Of course, they were the only girl couple there. Some of the girlfriends stopped to admire Toy's corsage and scan to see who her prom date was. When they saw her holding Rocky's arm they did a double take. It was no mistake. There was Rocky trying to look cool and trying to look like a boy for all the world to see.

Who did she think she was anyway? Everybody knew Rocky Corvair from last year. She was the girl always getting suspended and the only girl to drop out of St. Maria Goretti High School in 1967.

The girlfriends mumbled, "Nice dress Toy," and ran to grab their dates. Behind Toy's back they whispered. "The nerve of her ruining our prom by bringing that Rocky Corvair. A girl! Can you imagine? How did Rocky think she could just walk in here and we wouldn't notice her? And Toy, did you see that dress she was wearing? She looked like a slut with those black stockings, and you could see she had on black underwear underneath that dress. I always knew she had a bad reputation."

The crowd hushed when they saw Sister Alice and Mother Superior heading across the gym.

They were over by the punch bowl when Mother Superior grabbed Rocky by the ear, took Toy by the arm spilling her punch over her 36-C, and escorted them out the door. She would be contacting their parents and would deal with Toy directly first thing Monday morning!

Poor Toy and Rocky. They had dressed their finest and now they had to leave. Toy was visibly upset. Not only did she have punch juice on her new dress, but now the tears were spilling over onto her new chest, and the foam was coming out of her bra.

All Rocky could think about was getting her into the back seat of her Malibu. "C'mon Toy, you look fine. You were the best dressed girl there, and I love you for it."

All Toy could think about was getting suspended from school. This was her senior year and she looked forward to graduation, marrying Rocky, and going to the beauty academy.

Rocky took out a handkerchief to wipe the tears. This made Toy cry even more. Rocky jammed her hands into her pockets. She felt helpless and looked it.

"What'd I do now?"

"Baby, you're ruining my mascara."

Rocky pleaded. "Well look, I'm sorry. It's not my fault they didn't want us there. Look Toy, don't let them ruin our good time. I got some money and gas in the car. We can drive down the shore and get a hotel room. If you don't want to stay out all night we can park somewhere and dance to our own music."

Toy was sorry. Rocky was being so sweet, and she did want to be with her. And Rocky was right. She really was the best dressed girl at the prom, and Rocky definitely looked better than the dates those pompous bitches came with.

That night Rocky and Toy ended up parking at the edge of the river bank. Rocky's new expertise was unhooking Toy's bra with one hand while the other massaged Toy's thigh. Toy contented herself by watching Rocky's hand climb higher and higher until it reached her panties, which were clinging to her by her own dampness. By the time Rocky had her hand inside, Toy was chewing furiously on her Doublemint gum, and as she climaxed bit Rocky's neck leaving a trail of doublemint from the nape of her neck to her shirt collar.

"Oh my god, oh my god!" Toy was crying as she came.

Rocky thought Toy had never had it so good and continued to slip her fingers in and out of her lover's juicy pussy.

What Rocky didn't know was that Toy was exclaiming over her gum, which was now lost in Rocky's hair.

It was a memorable night for both of them.

Riding the Cow

Sally Bellerose

In 1957 my father bought his first car and I learned to behave. The car was a wood-paneled Chevy wagon. It was brand new. I was a white brunette female. I was six years old. He loved us both. I learned to behave on the ride to Uncle Louie and Antie Bernice's farm in my father's '57 Chevy. My father drove the whole family to the farm every Saturday morning. It was hard to behave, especially in a car. I had no experience behaving in small moving spaces, but I had no choice. I wanted to ride the cow.

It's a long ride from Fairview to Granby. I listen to my father sing along with Doris Day, Roy Rogers and the double mint twins. He doesn't care who's on the radio, although he likes Perry Como best. The car radio only gets one station. I like the music but even at six I know that my mother is right when she says, "That's enough Dear, you'll make the children tone deaf." My father's voice isn't plain bad, it's painfully lousy.

I could block out his noise, the way I do when my baby sister starts to bawl in my ear as we sat side by side in the back seat, but my father always drags me into it. He presses his hand to his heart like he's been mortally wounded and asks, "What do you think, little girl. Is your Daddy's voice that bad?" My mother yells at him to keep his hands on the wheel.

It's important to keep both of my parents happy. Most of the time it doesn't matter so much. Neither one of them is very strict. When I'm bad they threaten to put me to bed early or not let me watch T.V. I like my bed and I always fall asleep when the T.V. is on anyway.

But on Saturday morning I want them happy. One time they had a fight on the way to the farm. They were fighting because my father wanted to take a puppy home from the farm and my mother didn't want to. After the fight we stopped to get an ice cream cone and went straight back home without even going to the farm. I cried. My father said, "It's O.K. We'll get you the dog." I didn't care if we got a dog or not. I missed my cow.

So this morning I'm being careful. If I say my father has a lousy voice he might get mad. If I say he doesn't have a lousy voice my mother might get mad. They probably won't get really mad, just teasing mad, but I'm not taking any chances. I want to be a good happy girl, with good happy parents, who let me ride my cow. I distract them from the dilemma of my father's lousy voice by reading the time aloud from the round green clock. If I sit up real straight I can see it from the back seat. It sticks out from the dashboard. My father is proud that there's a clock and a radio in his new car. My mother is proud that her six-year-old can tell time. If I hadn't volunteered the time my mother would have asked me before we got to the farm just to be sure I hadn't forgotten how. When we finally get there my father and Uncle Louie hang around the car admiring the whitewalls and the clock. They open the hood.

My mother, baby sister, Auntie Bernice and I sit around Auntie Bernices' big kitchen table. There's a plate of chocolate chip cookies on the table. I smell them before we even get out of the car, but I sit still and don't grab one. The first thing my Auntie Bernice says after she giggles my baby sister around for a while is, "What time did our little girl get to Auntie Bernices' today?" She winks at my mother.

My mother takes my baby sister, bounces her confidently on her knee and says, "Go ahead honey. Tell your Auntie what time it says on the clock."

I'm confused because the clock says the wrong time. The big hand is on the twelve and the little hand is on the four. We haven't had lunch yet so it's still morning. I say, "Your clock is broken." My mother beams.

Auntie Bernice is happy too. She says, "Well, what time does it say honey?"

I say, "Four o'clock."

My mother kisses my baby sister, who squeals. My Auntie gives me four chocolate chip cookies. Everybody is happy. Uncle

Louie and Auntie Bernice have a big farm, my father has a shiny car, my mother has a giggly baby and a daughter who can tell time. I'm pretty sure it's almost time to ride the cow.

Uncle Louie and my father come in. Auntie Bernice tells them how she changed the clock to trick me. Uncle Louie picks me up and looks at auntie Bernice, "Now, Mother, you should know by now that you can't trick this little lady." She's not his mother. I asked him one time. He laughed and told everyone that I thought Auntie Bernice was his mother. On the way home that day my mother wasn't happy. She said I shouldn't ask such questions. She said some day Auntie Bernice would be blessed with children and I should behave until then. Uncle Louie and Auntie Bernice don't have any kids. They have cows and horses and chickens. Maybe he thinks if he calls her mother they'll get some kids.

Uncle Louie sits me down on the counter. I like jumping down off the counter, but he stands there in front of me, so I can't. I want to poke him but I sit there behaving, staring at his belly until he lifts me off again. He pats me on my bottom and says, "Go talk to Molly." I run out of Auntie Bernices' kitchen. The screen door slams, but no one yells at me.

I push the latch up with both hands and the barn doors swing open. The cows are all standing in their stalls. Forty-seven cow heads turn toward me. They think I'm going to let them out to pasture, it's almost time. I run to Molly's stall. I hang on the rail and scratch between her eyes. She looks at me lovingly with her big crossed eyes. She lowers her head a little and I scratch behind her ears. I listen to hear if the men are coming. It's hard to listen. You have to stand on your tiptoes and strain your ears to hear above the cow noises. I don't hear their voices or their footsteps so I climb up the side of the stall onto Molly and straddle her wide back. My legs stick out in opposite directions across her. I hug her neck and tell her how much I love her. She says, "Moo." I hear my father and Uncle Louie outside the barn and climb off Molly.

My father compliments Uncle Louie on how clean the place

is. Uncle Louie lets me lead Molly out onto the pasture. He picks me up under my armpits. He lifts me up off the grass and sits me on the cow. Uncle Louie makes me sit with both my feet hanging down over one side of her fat belly. He thinks that's how you ride a cow. He stands there smiling. He never lets go of me. He's nice to me and he smells like the barn. He smells like a clean cow, but I wish he would go away.

Mama yells from the kitchen window, "Don't be scared honey. Louie, don't you let her fall off that cow." Uncle Louie's hands are big. They reach all the way around me. I want him to go away so I can sit on the cow the good way, with my legs apart. Mama says I'm too small to ride the cow with one foot on one side and the other foot on the other side. She says it's dangerous because my legs are so short and the cow is so fat. That's stupid. I bet it's easier to fall off a cow with both legs hanging over one side than it is to fall of a cow if you're riding it with your legs apart. I want to learn to ride the cow the good way so that I can teach my friends, the twins, how to ride a cow.

I named the cow Molly. Uncle Louie let me pick out a cow for my very own and I picked Molly. I'm the only one she lets on her back. Uncle Louie says Molly lets me ride her because I'm such a speck of a girl. It's really because Molly loves only me. She'll love the twins too, when she gets to meet them. I have a plan. I plan to behave and make my parents so happy that they'll say yes next time and take the twins to the farm with us and we'll all ride Molly. Uncle Louie holds on to me and my father walks Molly around the pasture with me on her back. Molly and I pretend that Uncle Louie fell in a gopher hole and my father has to help him climb out. It takes them all afternoon and Molly and I ride all around the pasture alone for the rest of the day.

But it's not really true; Uncle Louie squeezes his hands together and lifts me off Molly. Sometimes Uncle Louie pretends he can't tell time. He asks me to read his watch for him. Sometimes I think I'll fool him and say it's only been one minute since I got on the cow so he has to let me stay on longer, but I know he can really tell time by himself.

I could tell time when I was five. When I was five the twins, Suzzie and Jenny Wallowitcz moved into the house next door. Mama said, "Tell Mrs. Wallowitcz what time it is." I said "It's 2 o'clock," and Mrs. Wallowitcz said, "What a smart girl." Now the twins Suzzie and Jenny Wallowitcz can tell time and Mrs. Wallowitz doesn't think I'm so smart anymore.

I'm the one who showed the twins how to tell time. Mrs. Wallowitz says that's not true. She says the teacher taught them on the big clock at school. It is true. I showed the twins how the little hand moves. I told them just to pretend that the big hand wasn't there. We were lying on my bedroom floor. I was in the middle holding the alarm clock I gave them for their birthday. They have the same birthday. The twins pushed up against me to see the clock and we turned the knob and made it all different times. The big hand was too hard for the twins to read. The twins still don't know how to read the big hand.

The twins wear shirts with no sleeves. Sometimes when it's hot they don't wear any shirts. I always have to wear a shirt, except in the tub. It was very hot the day I taught the twins to tell time, but we were playing at my house, so we had to keep our shirts on. I'll teach them the big hand at their house.

Once I slept over at the twins house and we wore Mr. Wallowitcz's t-shirt. It was so big that it fit all three of us at the same time. Then Jenny got out and put on Suzzie's babydoll pj's on top of her own babydoll's and there was more room for me and Suzzie inside Mr. Wallowitcz's T-shirt. Suzzie stuck her head out of one of the sleeves and I stuck my head out of the other sleeve. I asked Suzzie if I could be a twin too and she said yes, but Jenny said no. I bet Jenny would let me be a twin if I let her ride the cow.

Now it's 8 o'clock at night. I'm home in my stupid pj's. They make me wear stupid pj's with sleeves and legs on them in bed. It's dark outside. They won't come to bed until 10 o'clock. Jenny and Suzzie get to stay up on Saturday until Mr. and Mrs. Wallowitcz go to bed. Then they get to wear sleeveless babydolls, but I don't care because I'm going to ride my cow. Saturday nights are the best nights to ride because I almost always get to see Molly on Saturday mornings. Sometimes I don't put the clothes I wore while I was sitting on her back in the hamper like I'm suppose to. I roll them up and hide them under my bed. I take them out when it's time to ride. I put my head on them and they smell like Molly. I pull up the sleeves and the legs of my pj's. They bunch around my armpits and between my legs. Tonight I have a long time to ride. Sometimes it takes a long time before the blanket and sheets I pull up between my legs get to be my cow. Tonight it's easy.

I throw one leg over my covers and lie on my side. I ride with one leg on one side and one leg on the other side, like you're suppose to ride. I pull on the reins and the saddle pushes in to the big crack below my belly button. No one knows that my sheets become Molly's secret cow saddle and secret cow reins. Even Mama and Uncle Louie don't know. They think that reins and saddles are only for horses. Uncle Louie keeps telling me that when I'm bigger I can ride his horses. I'm never going to ride Uncle Louie's horses.

The harder I pull on the reins the faster Molly goes. Cows can go fast if they want to. I squeeze my bottom and feel my two asses. Jenny and Suzzie have three different names for their bottoms. Asses is the best one. I like to feel Molly pulling up the middle of my asses. When she starts to run fast she makes two of me. Two me's, both the same. Two asses and two legs and two arms and two eyes. Two sides just the same. I've got an extra everything.

I think it's funny that I have an extra everything, two me's. I squeeze my bottom harder and giggle. I don't giggle loud because I don't want my mother to come in to find out if everything a alright. I squeeze from the hole in the back to the hole in the front. I pull Molly's reins. I think it would be fun if I could squish my two me's together. Molly likes it too. I'm going to tell the twins there's four of them. I squeeze and squeeze. I squeeze me and me and Suzzie and Suzzie and Jenny and Jenny. Molly runs faster, faster. The cow bell dingle dingles. I hold on tight to her reins and grab her neck to stay on. I'm a little scared but Molly talks to me in her cow voice, "Don't be scared, honey." I squeeze into myself. Faster, faster, we go me and me and Molly and Molly and the four twins. We hang on to each other tight and we ride very fast and very far, the good way.

A Casual Affair: A Very Short Story

Ayofemi Folayan

Part I: The Kiss

The last time I kissed someone caught me totally by surprise. She had just hugged me outside the restaurant - no awkward triangulations over steering wheel and drive shaft for us. As we pulled up outside the Center and I was turning to get out of the car, she pulled me back toward her and kissed me full on the mouth. A surge of fire flashed and exploded, then rumbled through my body like an unstoppable flow of molten volcanic lava. Before I could shut off that feeling, the intense shocking surprise of it like a splash of ice water on my face, she grabbed my head and pressed her mouth once again on mine, which opened slowly, like the delayed lens of a camera, and welcomed the warm breathy moistness of her tongue. Still in shock, I felt time slam on the brakes, and the force reverberated into my clit, swelling and throbbing. Desperate, I could not breathe or think, I could only respond, getting wetter, the moisture welling up from a spring I thought had gone dry: tears from my eyes, sweat from my pores, passion through my vagina. I grabbed the car door handle, as if it were the side of the pool when I still didn't know how to swim. And in grabbing the door, I released the powerful suction, gulped in a disappointingly cold gasp of air, and slid out of the car onto the sidewalk, my feet like sponges and my head like the perfect meringue on Aunt Rubinetta's lemon pie.

"Call me," she whispered, and I nodded, not trusting myself to speak.

Part II: The Dream

I am consumed by a passionate desire to make love to her. I wake up with fire coursing through my groin, the hot flames melting my resistance to the potential for joy she represents. In my dream, I re-write Friday morning the way I wished it had been. I come into her room, the sunlight filtering through the window and leaving golden touches sparkling in her hair. She is curled into a human question mark under the covers of her bed. I lift the covers and lie down beside her, when suddenly I notice that we are both naked and I can feel the warm caress of her skin against me. I gently kiss her neck, her hair, and the spot between her shoulder blades, until she stirs, sleep making the sounds coming from her throat soft and husky. She rolls over and allows me to kiss her neck and the skin above her breasts and her eyelids. Wondrously, I find her mouth and the soft sweetness of her lips. As I kiss her mouth, she snuggles deeper into my embrace and I feel the heat from her body warming the coldness in my heart that has longed for this moment. She arches her back and opens her mouth to the tender teasing of my tongue.

I realize I don't know what gives her pleasure, and more than anything I want to bring her great joy, so between kisses, I say, "Sweetheart, I want you to have everything exactly as you want it. Talk to me about what you want. Feel free to ask me for anything that will give you pleasure." At first, she is shy about giving me specific information, but I make it extremely clear that I will only proceed when she has given me instructions. She whispers in my ear that she wants me to suck her breasts, which gives me great joy, to be able to specifically do something she wants. My mouth is hungry for the tender taste of her breasts, and I suck them and lick them and kiss them until the nipples are firm and erect.

She begins to writhe against me, and I ask if there is something else she desires. "I want your mouth on my clit," she informs me. So I gradually slide along her body, nibbling and kissing little places that call to me for attention, until my chin feels the ticklish sensation of her pubic hair. I stop and bury my face deep in her vagina, rubbing my whole visage in slow circles against her clit until she begins to moan, and then I begin to gently lick and suck her clitoris. Then, as my own passions increase in intensity, my tongue works faster until she starts rocking with the rhythm of her approaching orgasm. Against my chin,

I feel the slippery wetness of fluids seeping from her vagina and slip my fingers inside her. I probe deep with my fingers until I find the "G" spot as her moans get louder and her body grabs my hand and she rides out the tidal wave of her orgasm. She grabs my head as if to pull me away, but I am transported into the rhythm of her tsunamic orgasm and begin slow gentle licks with my tongue to bring her back on the high tide of a second orgasm. Her sweet succulent flesh yields subtle flavors as I suck on her tenderly, trying to coax another hot flash of passion from her. I shudder as my own clitoris boils in the hot flush of my impending orgasm, and I grind against her knee, trying to scratch my itch. I feel the surge of our mutual orgasms, as waves crash through both our bodies and drop us on soft sands, where we hold each other. I wrap my arms around her and kiss her gently, on her eyes, her cheeks, her lips, her neck, her ears, her hair, and tell her how special she is to me, what a precious gift she is and making love with her is. We fall asleep holding each other, and our bodies bake in the afternoon sun, as if we truly are on a private beach somewhere.

I wake up and marvel at this wonderful vision, and I long to feel the soft curve of her ass against me, the gentle mound of her breast pushing against the hairs on my arm, and know that I want more than this dream.

Part III: The Sex

A throbbing pulse drives my heartbeat and paces the new hunger, the deep desire I feel. Hot, wet, ravenous juices boil in my vagina, as sizzling rare steaks on the grille of my passion wrap around her hand, toast its surfaces in their molten heat, and greedily suck her in deeper and deeper, until she can scratch the surface and strike the match which will ignite the dynamite of my orgasm.

Hungry, ravenous, voracious, aching and pleading, come into me, fill me, feed me, give me what I have wanted for a long time. The juices spatter and sizzle, as I writhe in a passionate dance of ecstacy, pleasure and power.

I tilt my head way back, open my mouth, and a scream rockets into the space above us, whirling around our throbbing bodies like a gyroscope, weaving and spinning, reeling and grinning. How magnificent I feel in this instant makes no sense, my body floating above its usual pain on cushions of passion and promise. "Please, don't stop!" I beg, and like a lap swimmer hurl my body back into the thrashing tide and wildly pull myself toward the distant wall of the pool.

"Baby, baby, baby!" I groan as the earthquake snaps, slamming me against the bed, then rolling and heaving me toward the stable island of refuge just beyond the last wave of my orgasm. I laugh, a rising tide of sound, a carillon cresting on the high sweet note of joy I feel as I am beached after the final orgasm fades, panting and sweating as salty drops of sweat drain onto the gritty sheets. "Baby, please!" I holler, more for the release it provides than any real desire to communicate.

My eyes finally stop spinning and my eyelids roll open in an expression of surprise. "How do you do that to me?" I ask, astonished.

Baby

Janet Silverstein

Her name is Baby. She's six feet square and about three feet deep. I'd been admiring her fine lines, her blue depths, her redwood casing for months. I'd stand in front of her, stroking the smooth surface, could just imagine myself naked under the stars, the wind ruffling the palm trees, the steamy air rising in a cloud around me. And the jets. What could I do with those jets? So I did it. It was the thought of the jets that convinced me to take the plunge of course. After all, a little bit of debt, or even a moderate amount, never really hurt anyone.

I took the day off from work to watch her be installed. When they banged her coming off the truck, I screamed, "Be careful with her. She's delicate you know and I'm counting on her." You can imagine what that was like, watching this male harm Baby before she was even settled in. He gave me an odd look but he was more careful after that. They lifted her gently and carried her into the backyard. They poured the cement under the bottle brush tree and gingerly laid her into her new home. Wires were run from the house, under the ground, back out and attached to her side. Her motor was functional. I was losing control because of this intense anticipation so I ran into the house for a quick cold shower.

By the time I came back out, she had four inches of water in her. The brute that had handled her so roughly told me she'd be full in a few hours and hot by tomorrow and left. I yelled over the fence, "Tomorrow? Why not tonight? Please make it tonight! Please!" He gave me another strange look, slammed the door of his truck and roared away.

I went back to Baby. I just wanted to check and make sure she was handling the influx of water all right. You can certainly understand that. I walked all the way around her, trailing my fingers along her blue sides, stroking her, making her welcome. I went to the water valve and opened it the rest of the way hoping that if she'd fill faster, maybe she'd heat up faster. I stood and watched the water flow from the hose into Baby. She looked lovely half filled with water.

It was hard to be patient. Waiting and watching as the water level rose from half to three quarters full seemed to take days. But I was patient and eventually she was full.

I turned on the heater as soon as I shut off the water. She was frigid. Not exactly what I had in mind. I turned the heater up to maximum and closed her cover thinking that would heat her up more quickly, keep the warmth right inside her. Every ten minutes, well maybe every three minutes, I'd lift the edge of the cover and gently lower my hand into her wet insides. Still cold. Each time, she was still cold. I'd think that it was noticeably warmer and close the cover. But when I'd open it back up (three minutes later) she was still cold. You know it's hard to maintain a sensory memory of thermal units. Time passed. Slowly. There are an incredible number of three minute intervals in an hour, twenty to be precise. In two hours there are sixty and in three hours, ninety. She was still just barely warm. I went out for dinner. A watched pot never boils and all that.

I walked in the front door and out the back door and headed directly for Baby. She was beyond tepid. Definitely warm. Even beyond lukewarm. I lifted my leg over her edge and lowered my foot into her swirling waters. Warm. Not steamy hot. Not turn your skin lobster red. You know what I mean, warm enough to be soothing, to be gentle and soothing. I stripped off my clothes in three movements and hoisted myself onto her ledge. My feet dangled, just barely caressing the surface of Baby's waters. My fingers stroked her slick, solid side. I lowered myself slowly to the seat below me, sat on the bench and reached for the button. The red filtered light shone eerily in the cloudless night.

I stretched toward the other button. Bubbles. Bubbles bursting through the surface of the water, percolating through the small perforations scattered across her. They exploded with soft pops, the sound of the motor creating a background harmony.

The button again. The bubbles stopped and the jets started. Hard streams of water flowed from each of Baby's four sides. I shifted position so that my back was inches from the insistent stream of water. She massaged my lower back. I slunk down further on the seat as the jet of water stroked its way up my spine.

The button again. The bubbles returned but the jets remained. Baby started to emit steam. Clouds of misty air surrounded my head. The moon and stars were visible through the blanket of fog. I relaxed against Baby's silky sides, her hardness rubbing along my back. The bubbles exploded all around me, erratically emerging from behind my neck, under my arms, between my thighs. Her jet at my back was rotating wildly in a circular pattern. The stream of water remained in one spot for a few moments then swung ninety degrees, remained still for a moment then swung a full three sixty. I could live right here. Just soak until my skin puckered into nothingness.

The cloud of steamy air around my head grew steadily thicker, more dense. The torrent of water pounded against my back. The bubbles kept my nerve endings on red alert. All this stimulation, all this heat, all this moisture was becoming overwhelming. I shifted to Baby's other side, the stationary jet. I lowered myself onto the lounge bench beneath it. I rested with my ears just under the surface of Baby's waters. The bubbles exploding all around me echoed in my ears. The vibrations of the motor kept a gentle undulation going beneath me. The stream of water spurted across my hips.

Maybe you're sitting there, or lying there, imagining me rolling to my side, spreading my legs. Perhaps stretching my left leg to the other wall of Baby's side, my right leg bent at the knee, the jet of water caressing my inner thighs. Possibly you're picturing my hand reaching down and separating my lips, providing easy access for the hard, pulsing waters. Maybe you're hearing a small gasp escape from my mouth, seeing my tongue licking across my lower lip. Perhaps you see my other hand reaching for my breast, squeezing the nipple just slightly or tentatively pinching it, just a little. Do you see my hips lifting off the bench, pushing me closer against Baby's wall, against Baby's jet? My hips are moving faster, my hand spreading my lips as wide as possible, my fingers rolling my nipple between them. Maybe you think I'm lying there fantasizing about a woman, a woman going down on me, her tongue the jet, my hands hers. Perhaps you can see her long brown hair whirling in the waters around me or maybe you can just see Baby, me and Baby squeezing together. Perhaps you're hearing it now, the "Yes, Baby, yes. More, Baby. Oh baby, that's it. Yes, that's it." The scream muted because of the neighbors. My hips slowing down, my tongue gliding across my lips, my fingertips stroking the skin of my breast and you can see it in your mind.

Is that what you've been thinking? Is that what you imagined I would do with those caressing warm waters, those stimulating bubbles, the vigor of Baby's jets? But maybe I didn't roll over to my side. Perhaps I just laid there on the bench with the water streaming across my hips. Maybe the warmth of the waters lulled me, made me sleepy, caused all of the tightness in my muscles to seep into her waiting waters. Perhaps I just laid there for a bit, yawning and stretching, then sat up, pressed each button, got out and bid Baby good night. Maybe we needed to get to know each other better first. Maybe I don't do things like that on my first date, even if it is with a machine. After all, her name may be Baby but she's certainly not an innocent. Not the way I am.

Peppermint Candy

for Cynthia Dettman, in celebration of her 41st birthday, and her 10th anniversary of lesbianhood.

Elissa Goldberg

You should have seen Pearlie's eyes. "I'll have a peppermint," was all I said, and her blue eyes expanded like hot-air balloons. I waited. I drew in another breath, then said it again. "I'll have a peppermint now. Please."

I wasn't asking. I was telling. And Pearlie knew, 'cause after she'd looked at me for a long moment, she laid her cards down and pushed the candy dish over to me. First I took one, then she did. Then we sucked on our candies and stared hard at each other. It was two o'clock in the afternoon.

We didn't usually say it that way. You see, most times Pearlie'll say, "Want a peppermint?" and raise her eyebrows just above the rim of her glasses. Or sometimes I'll say, "How about a peppermint candy, dear?" That's our signal. We're old ladies. Our juices don't flow as easily as they used to. But a peppermint candy will get your mouth going, and the rest is easy from there.

The reason for the difference: that was the day Dorothy Hatter died. Shirley Wilkes had called in the morning. I knew even before Pearlie told me that it was a death call. They come often enough these days. One or the other of us is always putting that telephone receiver down, and keeping her back to the other before mustering her voice to say the news. When Pearlie told me it was Dorothy Hatter, we both stared out the window. The air was quiet for a long time.

Well, Pearlie made the first move. I'm sure you could say that I did because of my candy remark. But Pearlie-girl was the first one to leave the kitchen. "See you in a minute," she said, and then disappeared into her bedroom.

That's the next step. Forty-plus years we've been doing this, (only the past ten with peppermint candies, mind you), and Miss Pearlie is not about to amend her ways. She goes into her bedroom. I step out of her apartment, and cross the hallway to my own. Now, in any usual circumstance, this would be going on around nine o'clock in the evening, way past any busy neighbor's bed-time. No problem for one of us to pad across that hall, wearing a nightgown and bathrobe, carrying a toothbrush, you know, and all that.

This, however, happened to be during the middle of the day. As soon as I was inside my own home, I lost my determination. I didn't know what to do. Azalea Franklin right next door. The Westovers down the hall. And none of them too deaf. I walked to my closet, opened the doors. Then I closed them. Then I opened them again before I went to sit on my bed. Lately, I've been getting dizzy when I have to decide something. But I already told my doctor, I said, "You are <u>not</u> giving me pills for this condition, young man." Then I smiled real nice, because it isn't his fault he doesn't know about old ladies.

Pearlie knocked on my door then, and stuck her head inside. "Fern," she said. She was already in a bathrobe, and I could see her flannel nightgown beneath. She was raising her eyebrows real high. "Did you want to change your mind?" she asked.

"Pearl," I said, looking straight at her. "It's the middle of the day."

She cocked her head at an angle, and I could see her chin that's gotten all soft and hangy. "Well," she said, "I'll just go change then." Her lips were in that given-up expression, a straight stretch across to her cheeks. But she didn't leave the room. We just stared at each other, looking way through each other's faces to memories of other times. Our trip to Mexico. Pearlie in a bathing suit. The time she dressed as a man in order to take me out dancing on the Hilton ballroom floor to mark our twentieth anniversary.

"No," I said. "I'll be there right soon." She left then, and I unbuttoned my blouse.

I met Pearlie during the war years. She had a young son, a

husband in the Pacific, and a stopped-up sink. Me, I was working then as a plumber. Hard to find in those days, all the men somewhere else. I had my daddy teach me everything he knew. And it was a right nice way to get to know my neighbors. I'd go from having a cup of coffee next door to a biscuit down the street, and all that.

In those days, Pearlie was about a head and more taller than me. We'd been talking, telling one another small stories. After I gathered my tools, crouched down low, I stood up right into a most satisfying chest. And arms that didn't walk away. That sink, I'm telling you, it's kept us going for many, many years now, right through the news from the telegram, right through my daddy's funeral and then her daddy's funeral. Right through all this time to these apartments, across the hall from each other, answering the telephone calls again and again.

By the time I opened the door to Pearlie's bedroom, (nobody having witnessed my journey), she was already in bed, propped on two pillows and reading a book. The bedclothes were pulled up to her chestline.

"Hi," I said. Pearlie didn't say a word.

I climbed into bed beside her. Pearlie found a bookmark and put her book on the nightstand. I traced the outside of her ear with my finger, and then again with my tongue. With my eyes shut, my hands found those warm, familiar spots through her nightgown, her waist, the inside of her thighs, the stretched-out skin just beneath her belly-button. She pulled my face to hers with both of her hands. Her hands are stone smooth, like they no longer have finger-prints. She put her mouth on mine and kissed me. Felt like she was opening me up with her tongue, slow-like, full of love and peppermint, and that's when I had to stop. Soon as she'd opened me up to my throat, I pulled away.

"Wait," I said. I tried to clear my throat, but it didn't work.

You see, Dorothy Hatter was the only one who knew. She lived on the floor just above us, and stopped in occasionally with gossip news, or a bag of farm peaches. Always had a worried look on that thin face of hers, her eyes blinking away. One time she stopped in after Pearlie and I had just had a fight. There was still probably that close air between us, the kind that hangs about two people who're still settling down after a storm. She came in talking, but stopped in mid-sentence, looking from one to the other of us. For a moment her face lost its lines, and her eyes stopped blinking. She was taking it all in. When she continued talking, her voice was slower, but she kept on with her same original topic like nothing had changed.

She never said a word about it. Not to us. Not to nobody. But even so, just having her know made her sort of an anchor for Pearlie and me. Now she was gone, we were drifting free.

"Pearl," I whispered. "Take your nightgown off."

Pearl froze. See, this wasn't something we normally did either. Took off our nightclothes only after things had been good and warmed up, and only with all the lights out. "Why?" she said with big eyes.

"I want to see you," I said. We were both whispering.

She looked down at her ribbon, tied in a bow. Then she looked at my chest, all bundled in my nightgown. She nodded her head with her lips closed. "Okay," she said. But before she touched her clothes, she put her glasses back on.

We unsnapped our nightgowns. Those kind are easier for old ladies, don't have to lift your arms upside your head, and all that. Pearlie stared at me from behind those glasses. I felt nervous. In all the years we'd been together, we hadn't once looked at each other close up, If you know what I mean. It was winter outside, but Pearlie's bedroom was warmer than I'd ever felt before. We didn't have even bedsheets on us. And the only light came from the window, gray, cloudy light.

I looked at Pearlie. First at her eyes as they were taking me in. Then her shoulders. Pearlie'd been a strong old girl, and even now, you could see her muscles still there, just a bit on the saggy side is all. Her breasts, though, looked exactly as I knew them in my head, round and loose and welcoming, with skin you just want to roll into again and again.

"Mmmm," I said, and took off her glasses.

"Mmmm," she said, reaching behind me and pulling me to her by the small of my back.

"You're pretty strong for an old lady," I said.

"Shhh," she said. "It's three o'clock in the afternoon."

Slut and Prude Go To The Seashore #47

K.Linda Kivi

"Why is it that you need to expose yourself?" I asked Slut as I clicked a first shot of her lying naked in a crevice of the massive rock.

"Why is it that you need to hide the body you were born with?" she responded fixing her eyes on the camera lens. A great curl of ocean water smacked the thigh of the rock shoreline below. Above, chalky clouds crashed into leaden ones, writing storm warnings out for those of us below.

We had come to the open, stormy sea over the rise of heathery mauve that shelters the village where we live from the harsher elements. Yet, it was on days like these, when the zealous salt waves dragged at the granite shoreline, that I most wanted - no needed - to be outside.

I had brought my camera, carrying it bandolier over my shoulder. Slut had lagged behind, dragging her feet and cradling the menstrual weight of her breasts in her arms. She had wanted to loll in the claw-foot tub and nurse her cramps, but I hadn't let her. In exchange, I said nothing as she dressed however she wanted to, in layers of thin colourful cotton and a myriad of scarves. At least she had agreed to wear a bra for a change.

We hadn't talked as we clambered over the smooth and cutting edges of the rock mass. Only the ocean gaped its hairy mouth as cormorants and gulls dipped down towards it.

Slut and I had stayed high on the rocks as we made our way, like usual, toward the point. There, a curve of rock guards the entrance to the village harbour and juts out into the sea. It was there that I liked to sit and photograph the crazed sky.

Why was it that I agreed to take Slut's picture that stormy Sunday morning? Normally, I photograph rock, water and sky, gulls and sea creatures, fly-eating pitcher plants and scrubby heather, but not people, certainly not Slut with her kinky ideas and lavish body. How did she talk me into it?

"So will you?" she asked me. "After all, I humoured you by coming out here at all."

"I guess so." She had a point. But what was it? Suddenly it occurred to me. She didn't want a picture to send to her mother. No. That she had other ideas quickly became apparent.

Slut had found a fold of coral coloured rock that, in her eyes, resembled female anatomy.

I eyed the curves of the smooth, pink rock with folded arms.

What came next? With Slut, you never could tell. She started to unravel her wind tangled scarves. It took me a moment to realize that she was undressing, taking everything off, and that she wanted to be photographed naked. I should have known.

"Get dressed," I had commanded, irritated.

"No. Take my picture," she had countered.

"Come on Slut. What if someone comes along?" I even made a plea to her good sense. "And what about the storm?"

"Shut up Prude, so what if someone comes along. We've been rained on plenty before."

I had decided not to argue. From the safe haven of the view finder, I fiddled with the aperture setting, the focus, and when a blast of wind tore around me, I steadied the tripod. The storm was picking up.

Back on the rock, Slut unleashed her breasts and they tumbled out of her bra, liberated, as she would say. She stepped out of her underwear and I caught her peering intently at the reusable flannel pad that was stained crimson.

A cormorant sailed past, barely beyond my arm's reach, quivering in the rising storm and I ran to the camera to snap a few shots. What had I agreed to, I couldn't help wonder? I shivered and I scrutinized the underbellies of the navy clouds on the horizon for signs of a downpour. They would probably hold their loads until they reached the shore.

"Well?"

I turned the camera eye back toward the rock crevice.

Slut had sprawled out and wriggled her bare body into a comfortable groove.

"Well what?" I asked, blushing in spite of myself.

"I'm ready to be ravished by your voyeuristic tool" she said. This was going to be difficult, I could tell, but I took the first shot anyway.

She repositioned herself and began to rock from side to side, her hand grazing over the smooth expanse of her belly.

She took my silence as a sign that she had the upper hand, and I immediately regretted it.

"I really don't understand," she said, wriggling her thick hips, "how you can pretend that you're not turned on? Any why?"

She swivelled her hips in a slow arc as if to test the smoothness of the rock beneath.

"Who's pretending?" I looked away. "Just because I think that there are better things to do than spend our energies on so-called sexual exploration, doesn't mean . . ." I struggled for the right words, ". . . it doesn't mean anything."

"Admit that you're turned on at least." I saw that she was going to push me further as her hand snaked toward her crotch.

"And that you enjoy women."

"Of course I enjoy women. You of all people should know that."

"Good. Now photograph."

The sky had darkened considerably. It was going to rain on us, I was sure of it.

Slut's hand moved again, slowly-slowly towards her crotch, and she threw back her head and let her dark hair tumble across the cool pink rock. "Come on," she urged, almost growling, "take my picture, girl."

"Okay, okay,"

Click. But I couldn't let her win. "Why is it, though, that you obsess about sex, about bodies, about relating?" I threw a little sarcasm into the final word.

She spread her legs a little. "The most potent obsession is denial."

Click. What can you say to that? Sometimes it's better to hold your tongue. Prude, better hold your tongue. And I did.

Her hand reached the edge of her curly bush, where her fingers began to twirl strands of hair into swirls. The wind reached too, into Slut's niche and goosebumps rose on arms. She moaned a little.

Click.

Click, click.

I don't know how she does it, on purpose or what, but she has a way of finding things that are just beyond the realm of acceptability. And each time, I'm surprised. I should have known she'd get kinky about her blood. I should have known. She curved the fingers of her left hand into her vagina and drew out a fingerful of blood.

"Here," she said and stretched her hand toward the camera.

"Here."

Click. "Put it on yourself. I dare you."

"No dare at all."

She spread her legs and drew her hand across her belly from her left thigh to her right breast, leaving a streak of brilliant red.

Click. There was nothing I could do except click.

She smiled at me and reached back down, pushing her hand deeper in. She pulled her hand out suddenly, with a gasp, and began to rub her hands together with the glee of a child first discovering fingerpainting. Her palms slid across each other and grew more and more red until the lines of her hands were wet with menses. Then, with the care of a print maker, she laid both her hands across her inner thighs and lifted them away.

The hands seem to say, "come touch me, come." Click.

CLICK.

The first drops of raining began to fall; her blood mingled with the water, streaking down the pink rock into the crevices that led to the sea. She put her hand back inside her vagina, this time more for her own pleasure than the camera's benefit.

Click. Her hair snagged in the rocks and pieces of moss flecked her skin. She pushed herself up, arched, balancing on her splayed feet and the backs of her shoulders as she thrust her hand in and out rhythmically.

Click. I had to catch my breath. Just snap those pictures Prude, I told myself, and you'll be alright. But it's raining, my sensible side complained, without talking my eyes off of Slut.

My camera could be ruined.

Just one more. YesClick. Just one more. YesClick, yesss.

Slut pulled one hand out and pushed the other in. With her free hand she rubbed circles around her nipples and then around her breasts and finally, around her whole belly, until she was slathered in red, in rivulets of blood.

We needed to go. To seek shelter. But I didn't think I could stop her. Click, click, click.

She changed hands again, this time starting a chant or a dirge or some kind of rhythmic moan that had no words. With her other hand, she reached to her face and smudged blood across her cheeks. She drew her fingers through her hair, she ran her index down the bridge of her nose. She sang louder. She sang harder.

Click. Oh, Slut. We've got to go, I wanted to cry out.

The burdened blue clouds were above us, as wild with wind and rain as she was with song and blood. They roiled above us and the birds huddled where ever they could find shelter.

But Slut was occupied, full of herself. Full.

I forgot to click.

I had to remind myself.

Click.

She was rocking and singing and smearing and pushing and pushing and gushing.

How much blood could one woman hold. It was not drying.

Like watercolour, it seeped across the canvas of her skin. She was marbled in swirls of crimson.

Click.

She turned, gnashing her teeth, moaning, onto her belly and the blood mingled with the coral of the rock. She rolled back and ground her bottom into the red she left there. She was entirely red, entirely wet and the storm was not going to hold for her pleasure. It was not going to hold.

"Slut!" I shouted over the wind, over her moans.

"Yessss!" she hissed.

"The storm!"

"Yessss. I'm coming. I'm coming." The syllables broke and stuttered as she arched higher and higher.

CLICK.

I finished the roll.

Click,

Click:

Click.

Oh . . .

I buried the camera under one of Slut's scarves and pulled her to her feet. We dressed quickly and ran.

We arrived under the cover of the front porch of my green house just as the deluge came. The rain fell in sheets of thunder, drowning the roar of the sea beyond with its pounding on the metal roofs of the village.

I shivered and went inside. I deposited my camera on the kitchen table with a sigh. My head felt large and heavy as though there was more space in there than usual. I unwrapped my sodden and bloody scarves and piled them on the kitchen table where they made moist, steamy mounds and a trail red droplets followed me across the kitchen floor. The bathroom door stood ajar and the magnificent claw-footed tub beckoned. I filled it, hot and high, to soothe my cramps and swollen breasts and when I climbed in, Slut and Prude left me to soak in peace.

Three Poems

Kate Berne Miller

No Music

This is a dance – a two-step, a waltz, a polka,
a bump and grind for us.
You dress for the occasion – sheer black, floor length –
the lines of your body
full fruit underneath.

I come naked to the scent of you –
warm musk and sweet oils. My hands slide
under your skirt, hunger for skin. My palms cup
the flesh of your ass –
there is no music.

I am eager to taste – feel my tongue caress
slick wet folds – suck the sweet center
down into me. You come in my mouth – the beat of you
rolling over me, wave after wave –
the whole ocean of you
mine for a moment.

Why I Don't Ride Greyhound Anymore

To the lover who broke up with me
on the white courtesy phone
in a greyhound bus station:
love poems written years after
are the best –
bittersweet as dark chocolate, sharp as the white flash
of your teeth.
You were my image in the mirror –
reversed.

My strongest memory – that winter storm
at the Oregon coast.
You riding me on the carpeted floor,
the fury of sleet and wind slashing the windows,
covering our moans.
You arched backwards, hair brushing my feet,
your taste – the wild ocean
in my mouth.

For years your long hair haunted me,
cascading across my face in dreams –
following me cross-country,
stuck to my belongings.
I thought I'd never find
a bite as sweet as yours,
or pull all your greying hairs from my heart –
but I have.

Sea Turtle

You are a wide, wide river
a high dive into deep water
eyes open
we slide
slippery as seals
salt – your lips
salt – your skin
salt wet – your sex
your tongue rimming my ear
breath hot, the full weight of you
length and width – animal heavy
and panting
caught in your stare –
I swim
and swim
and swim.

Almost A Love Story

Ruth Mountaingrove

I think I fell in love with her almost immediately. But then everyone did. I had heard rumors of this "wunderkind" who had shown up in summer school, bright, intelligent, with a keen sense of humor. An accelerated student fresh out of high school. Young. Too young I thought for me, an aging junior. Six years can make quite a difference in adolescence. A huge gap usually. Now that I'm nearly seventy, twenty or thirty years difference in age does not seem nearly as large.

I was in summer school that year not because I was failing but because I had screwed up my schedule and it was the only time I could pick up required courses. Being poor, I had to work all through that summer to pay for my room and board. So what with studying and working in the science labs and the greenhouse and running the darkroom I had little time for social life.

I only saw her once that summer. She was with a woman older than she was, but then we all were. They both had a way of looking at things that was refreshing in this stodgy college I was suffering through.

I was intrigued by her mind and overwhelmed by her beauty. That combination has always been my downfall. She was a commuter which meant that she arrived on the bus every morning and went back to the city every night. Sometimes her father would pick her up.

Why she was in this small backwater teachers college, I never figured out. I knew why I was there. I couldn't afford anything else. But she, she belonged in a private girl's college. She had class.

Perhaps it was the war. Millions were having their lives changed by the war. Her father seemed to want to keep her near him. I never heard her talk about her mother. Her brothers were in France in the Army. I never knew much about her background. To me she was an enigma, and all the more intriguing for that.

How we got to be friends I can't remember. I think she was in one of my classes because I remember her handwriting, a kind of printing that women from upper class schools seem to learn. I can still see the elephants she doodled on the side of her notes. I kept one of the drawings for a long time.

One of my jobs was in the visual education class where I taught the use of the Leica camera and the process of developing and printing in the darkroom. She was in that class.

Actually I wouldn't have had that job at all if it hadn't been for the war. This was always a man's job. And it went back to being a man's job after the boys came back to college but I was graduated by that time.

Since the college valued their expensive Leica very much and it was the only one they had, it was my job to take a student into the darkroom, have them load the camera's cassette in total darkness, then turn on the light while they loaded it into the camera. It went like this: we used bulk film that came in 300 foot lengths; you grasped the end of the film, held it to your nose with your left hand and with your right you unrolled the film as far as you could reach. At that length you cut it, re-wrapped the bulk film and put it back in the can, and began to load the cassette with the piece you had measured. The leica cassette was a piece of art. It had three pieces that fit into each other. All the pieces were machined brass. Sometimes I had to help the inept of either sex, but she had no trouble once the process was explained and went right ahead and loaded it.

On a beautiful sunny spring day we took the Leica out. I explained f-stops, depth of field, and the little gizmo that sat on top of the camera where the flash cubes sometimes are these days; the parallax corrector. This had a dial which you adjusted as you looked through its viewfinder. It was supposed to keep you from cutting off peoples heads. I explained the use of the triangles she saw as she looked through the camera's viewfinder, how she needed to bring both of these together to bring the camera into focus. And I explained the use of the exposure meter. Well all of this can be pretty intimate.

As we left the building she took photographs of blossoming trees. Then we went up in the tower of the main building, a dirty old place used mostly for storage, and she took views of the campus. The cupola was the highest place on campus, almost five stories high, and looking out of it you got the effect of being in a low flying plane. She took photographs there, too. And she continued taking photographs as we walked out into the country. I didn't teach composition but she proved to have a good eye.

We talked about school, about photography, about life. I was enchanted. Was it then that we began to discuss the book of Job, that strange book in the collection that Jung would devote a book of his own to? Later I would write a poem about our talks beginning:

"We bridged our friendship with the book of Job
Climbing the heights of ecstacy together."

I gave her a copy of the poem one day when she was in my college room and after she read it she blushed and saying she was late for class, ran out the door.

Job and his problems were the focus of many long discussions. The enigma of this god. Neither of us had much religion left, or belief, so it was an intellectual exercise tinged with sexuality.

After she finished the roll of film we took it back to the darkroom and I showed her how to load the daylight developing tank. She rewound the film, took it out of the Leica, fed it out of the cassette, closed up the tank and I turned on the light. From there it was a matter of temperature and time. We left the film to wash for a half hour and went out to sit in the sun and talk some more.

Then she left for class and I went back to the darkroom to look at the film. Not bad for a first time. I hung the film up to dry and went off to my own class.

There would be one more session when the student makes

five prints chosen from the contact sheet s/he has made. This would be done when the camera was not in use since the lens of the camera was also the enlarger lens. She made another appointment, made a contact sheet of her negatives, and selected five she wanted to enlarge to 5"x7" prints.

I set up the trays for her, as I did for all of the students, helped her set her negatives in the negative carrier, showed her how to change the amount of light by turning the ring with the f stops, and how to bring the negatives into focus by moving the head of the enlarger up or down by means of a large knob on the side.

It was all pretty elementary but with her in the room it was exciting. After all, darkrooms are just that – dimly lit with a red light – sensual. And she was excited, too, watching the print appear like magic out of the developer.

I was impressed with the prints she made. As photography editor for the current yearbook, I asked her to help me select photos; make a montage. We worked closely together, a good team.

The next year I became business manager and she became photography editor. We saw each other at yearbook meetings and sometimes got to talk. One day we took the Leica and went out for another walk in the fields. We took photographs of each other because she wanted a photograph of me. Of course I wanted one of her. I developed the film and printed photographs for both of us.

Some of my women teachers lived with each other. One of them, the Dean, who saw my lesbianism years before I did, warned me as well as she could and saw to it that even with all the overcrowded conditions in the dormitories due to the moving in of the air corps, I still kept my single corner room.

I was such an innocent. It took me ten more years to figure out who I was and by that time I was married and had three children. So was the "wunderkind." Married one of those college GI's.

We never slept together. I did sleep with other women and

you'll have to take that literally. We slept with each other in those narrow cots to stay warm in winter, to cuddle, and sometimes it was romantic, perhaps sensual, but for me, at least, it was never sexual.

I did feel sexual toward her. I wanted to be a man. I didn't really understand this but somehow I knew as a woman I didn't have the right to have these feelings. Besides I had a boy friend in the Army.

But one Saturday afternoon – did she have a Saturday class? – we were sitting in my corner room with its two long windows, one in the front of the building and one on the side. She was sitting next to the side window, sewing a button on her brown overcoat.

I was lying on my made bed. It had a Bates spread on it, all the rage for college dorms then, with pillows in the back so it could double as a couch.

We were talking about poetry, I think. I was trying to tell her how I felt about her, how ambiguous our friendship seemed to be. Whatever I was saying seemed to be working because she got up from the chair and came over and sat next to me on the bed, still working on that button. She was so close to me I held my breath as I would if a young fawn had come into my space. I did not want to frighten her off.

She finished the button. We were so close time stopped. I was totally aware of her presence. How long we stayed like that I don't know. And what might have happened I'll never know. Would one of us have touched the other? Broken through the paralysis?

She was paged over the loud speaker in the hall. It was her father come to pick her up. She jumped as though she had been caught out. Was that man psychic? As she ran down the hall she said we must continue this sometime. But we never did.

I still have those negatives stored in a round metal film canister somewhere in the Northwest, three thousand miles away from where they were taken. In these negatives we are forever young. It is always Spring.

Red Camisole

Berté Ramirez

As I recall it was an ordinary day, an okay evening. The movie was okay, white, heterosexual, but funny at least. Dinner was okay. We were in some sort of middle phase in our affair. The sex was great, but was it love? We had gone from every spare moment in bed to things less frantic, with more personality. Certainly more time for subtlety, more room for headaches, distractions, fatigue. The terrain was still uncertain, the lines of negotiation vague. Words like love and co-commitment waited like chorus girls at the edge of the stage for their musical cue.

She was charming enough that evening, her short short hair fragrant with some fancy mousse stuff. She was attentive, but still enjoying the moment, the world around her, the girl who took our order. We laughingly described lesbian seduction scenes with our favorite stars. I enjoyed looking at her, thinking my most fond recent memories and vaguely hoping tonight would be one of them. Ah, but my love cup gave me no read, damn. She was smiling, chatty.

It was already established that I would spend the night, so we proceeded in that direction. Kisses in the doorway, tea in the kitchen, easy comfort in the bathroom. She put on her ridiculous Father-Knows-Best pajama bottoms and a tank t-shirt that clung ever so nicely to her breasts. Missing tonight is the red silk camisole thing she wore our first night together. She knows and she knows I know she knows how delicious the silk feels against my skin, so much so that I would literally leap on her like a cat, rubbing my large breasts across her face and chest, whenever she wears it. Sometimes she wears a rough wool vest, equally delicious.

No, tonight it was the white T tank top. It was late. We both worked in the morning, both of us feeling that edge of the river, wanting to be swept away, but not alone, noooo . . . not alone. We snuggled, settling in spoon style beneath the covers, her warm breath on my neck, her bed redolent and rich with our safely spent passions.

I wanted her, but only if she wanted me. We were mature, polite, politically correct. We were women of color, in recovery, you name it we were recovering from it. I was on the verge of not getting my needs met. What if she wasn't in the mood? What if she said no? No, she's tired. No, she has to work. No, it's late, no, no, etc.

I lay perfectly still working through my thoughts like a cotton gin, somewhere between hell and the moment right now. She, however, has a mind like a clean sandy beach, always a little blue sky on those occasions when I am most likely to drone in my thoughts. She does, however, what she wants, when she wants and that is simply that.

She sighed and shifted closer. Gently she cupped my breast and nothing more. As if dreaming, sleepwalking (sleep-fondling?), she gently squeezes my nipple. I am immediately awash with hunger and satisfaction at the same time. My breath rises and falls with every circle her finger makes across my nipple. We are like this for some time, exquisitely so. She is patient, mysterious, spontaneous, waiting perhaps foolishly, not realizing what she does to me most of the time. Those chorus girls stamp their feet at the edge of the stage.

Her body wedges tightly against mine. No one's sleepy now. Warm and flushed with blood, I reach behind me to pull her yet closer. Quickly, as if that was her signal, she seeks out my inner lips, searching with her fingers until she feels how wet I am and gasps with pleasure.

Now I know she lost. Now I know she is mine, eager to feel all my wetness at once. I turn to her and we press together everything. Lips converge. Her perfume is like soup in my lungs. She will touch all my tender places. She will whisper, "Finish me, take me any way you like." And I will, several times.

But first she pulls away and lights a candle. She looks at me and softly approaches. She holds my face in her hands. Oh, this face," she says with obvious pleasure. Smiling, her eyes bolted to mine, she pulls out the red camisole thing from under the pillows. I hear a chorus girl twitter. I imagine the haggard, pale happy face I'll have in the morning when I finally make it to work.

The Letter

Toni Brown

It was midnight when Leslie stepped onto the mirror-walled elevator. The double doors closed with a muffled sucking sound and after its brief pneumatic wheeze, she was lifted toward the 15th floor.

Leslie scrutinized her appearance in the copper-tinted reflections and sighed. Frowning, she pulled at the ragged edges of her flat top hair-do. The high front was uneven, the sides were growing out and refused to lay close to her head. She mashed down the sides and back and gave her neck an unsatisfying rub. A haircut or perm was definitely in her future. She sighed again and tugged at the belt on her tan London Fog, suddenly uncomfortable with the rounded belly-bulge that obscured her waist. She took off the coat and draped it over her arm. She counted the floors as the illuminated numbers flashed on then off. She glanced at her watch. It wasn't that she didn't want to be home. It was just that she didn't look forward to it as much anymore. She hoped that Robin was asleep.

Leslie and Robin had been lovers for three months when they decided to move in together. They rationalized that since they spent all their time together anyway, Robin should move into Leslie's bigger apartment. Sharing one apartment was cheaper than keeping two, and they believed they could make *good* use of all the time they would save not riding the subway to each other's places.

At first, living together was all about the sex. They didn't spend *every* waking moment making love. It just seemed that way. If Leslie was washing the dishes, Robin stood close behind, her warm hands under Leslie's blouse. Robin would cup Leslie's large soft breasts in her palms and brush the hardening nipples with her thumbs. She would nuzzle past Leslie's collar to kiss her coconut-scented neck.

When Robin sat down to play her guitar, Leslie sat down beside her. She'd brush Robin's thick dreads aside and run the tip of her tongue along the edge of Robin's dark ears. Robin would beg her to stop and Leslie would slide to the floor, loosen and remove Robin's shoes and begin to massage her feet. Soon Leslie was kissing Robin's calves as her skillful hands traced their way up toward Robin's parted thighs.

Every Saturday night they would go dancing and danced only with each other. They called Anita Baker's "Sweet Love" and Chaka Khan's "Ain't Nobody" their special songs. What they did on the dance floor when these songs came on was almost too scandalous to watch. Their friends teasingly called it, "doin' the nasty."

When they came home, they continued their dance, entangled in each others arms beneath the flowered quilt Robin had made in high school home economics class. The next morning they held each other, weaving their plans and dreams together like the ribbons that joined the quilt's varied squares. Beneath the rumpled cover they blended their voices with the taste and smell of their love-making. Afterward Robin lit long tapers scented with myrrh "to invoke the blessing of the Goddess," she told Leslie. Leslie assured her that they already had.

The elevator stopped abruptly and the doors opened with a swish. Leslie stepped out onto the grey-blue carpet, turned left and started down the corridor of identical doors.

But in little more than a year, the magic of those sweet beginnings had somehow faded. They still washed dishes and played guitar. They just stopped touching each other as much.

Now, when they went dancing, since they had agreed that it was okay to dance with other women, Leslie found herself more often with strangers and friends than with Robin. Staying in bed all day gradually lost its charm. Going to work became a relief from the too long weekends with not enough to do. Somehow the passion between them had slipped away and was replaced with an uncomfortable boredom. Robin took a job volunteering at a local battered women's shelter three nights a week. Leslie switched to the evening shift at the "Taft Minimum Security Correctional Facility."

Robin began to read "Self Help" books designed to help couples put the "zing" back into their relationship. She waited for Leslie to come home to lit candles and soft music. She offered Leslie midnight snacks of sliced mango and white zinfandel. She rented erotic lesbian videos for inspiration. One night she met Leslie at the door wearing only a dildo in a black leather harness.

Leslie joined in the effort, bringing Robin freesia and irises for her bedside table. After a night of dancing, Leslie stopped the elevator mid-floor to make love to Robin against the polished walls. She read aloud from her poetry chapbook, while Robin soaked in a tub of scented oil and soap suds.

Inevitably the frequency of these adventures began to wane. Robin and Leslie began to discuss the concept of non-monogamy. They looked for a lesbian couples therapist.

Leslie pulled the ring of keys out of her pocket and selected the one she needed. Poised to push it into the lock, she saw a fat, lavender envelope with her name written in the center taped just below the peep hole. She pulled it down and opened it. Inside were many pages. Leaning against the wall in the dim light of the corridor, she began to read.

Sweet Babe,

Sorry I'm not there to tell you about this in person, but in my place is a woman, a very wonderful, very delicious woman. I say delicious as I have taken the liberty of tasting her just a little bit. (More on that later.)

Leslie stopped reading and checked the name on the envelope and the number on the apartment door. She wondered if she could be in the wrong building.

. . . La Tanya, I don't think you know her, came over to watch Cagney and Lacey reruns. I have to admit this wasn't the first time. She was over last week and the week before, too. I didn't mention it because, with you working so late, I enjoyed the company and felt kind of selfish about sharing it. (Sorry) Anyway, both nights she seemed to be spending more time watching me than Christine Cagney. So tonight I decided to ask her what the deal was.

She said she had a crush. Well, more like a "jones" than a crush. She used to see us at the clubs and got wet panties just watching us dance. She said, at first it was enough to just stand on the side and watch, but she got so into it she couldn't just stand there any more. She said she didn't know what it was we had but she wanted some of it.

So she found the courage to ask us to dance. (Separately of course.) She asked if I remembered when this happened. When I didn't, she reminded me. It was at the "Square." It was a slow dance. I remember because she held me so close I began to imagine that she was pressing her hips into me. I thought I was imagining it! I felt like I was melting into her. We continued our slow dance/embrace after the first song ended and well into the middle of the second and that wasn't a slow song! We jumped apart. She thanked me for the dance and disappeared into the crowd. I was shaking. I went looking for you. I remember telling you about it that night.

Leslie frowned up her face, trying to remember. She couldn't.

Anyway, she decided to lay her cards on the table. She said we had something, some kind of sensual energy that she could feel just watching us. When we danced with her she felt submerged in it. She could smell it, taste it. She went home and was obsessed by it, by us. She thought that if she just asked us to make love to her, really "doin' it" would end the crush and she could stop constantly fantasizing about it.

By this time we had come into my room and were sitting on my bed. I was showing her my "Great Black Women" postcard collection when she began to kiss me. So softly, so sweetly. I found myself sinking into the pleasure of it. But I asked her to stop. I told her that we have been having hard times, but I'm committed to my relationship with you and we are working very hard. She threw back her head and laughed. She said she didn't want to marry me, she just wanted to make love with me, tonight. No strings attached.

I've got to say I was tempted and Goddess knows I was turned on by her kisses, but she's not you, my lover. I told her as clearly as I could that I couldn't do it, wouldn't do it. But her kisses became more insistent and I felt myself slipping away.

She was wearing this pink, tailored button-down shirt and the first two buttons were loosened. I could see her blackberry nipple peeking out through the v-shaped opening. I unbuttoned two more buttons and I slipped my hand in.

She seemed to stop breathing for a moment, then kissed me so hard I thought I was going to pass out! Her hands were frantically pulling my shirt out of my pants. I began to lean her back to the bed, then the telephone rang.

She moaned when I got up to answer. My heart was pounding. I was sure it was you, that you had somehow sensed this was going on. It was the hot-line answering service. There was a woman in need of shelter and the woman on call couldn't be reached. I was "back up." I began to tuck my blouse in again.

When I returned to my room, La Tanya was naked and lying on my bed. I told her what had happened and that I had to leave. She arched her back. I couldn't help but want to touch her. She said she would wait for me to come back.

I began to argue, that it wasn't happenin', that you would be home soon. But she wouldn't hear it. She sat up, pressed her fingers to my lips and said, "Stop talking. I will wait for you to come back and quietly we'll make the kind of love I've been dreaming about. And Robin," she added, "if Leslie comes home first . . ." she raised her eye brows devilishly. I couldn't believe this was happening. I stood there transfixed, then I kissed her fingers and turned off the light.

So my love, in my room there is a woman in great need of your passionate talents. Please light all the candles around the room so that she will see you for the beautiful woman that you are. When she touches you, I know you will cry out with desire. She talked about making quiet love but I know she will join you singing your passion, blending your voices. As you reveal yourself to her, I have no doubt that she will know you for the wonderful lover that you are. You are *irresistible.*

All my love,

Robin

P.S. The dental dams are in the desk drawer.

Leslie pushed her key into the lock tentatively, as if she didn't really believe it would work, and turned it. The door fell open and she entered the living room. It was lit with more tapers than she had ever seen. The thick smell of amber/myrrh blended with the hot candle wax tickled her nostrils. Robin's bedroom door was open and the darkness inside seemed velvety. Leslie dropped the letter and her coat on the carpet and locked the door behind her. She picked up a candle and shielded it with her palm as she walked toward Robin's door.

In the bedroom, naked under her quilt, Robin smiled with wicked anticipation and waited for Leslie to come.

Milk

Susan Stinson

Martha picked up the pitcher and poured water into the basin. I watched the painted flowers on the bottom as they sharpened under the water. She sat down on the chair across from me and unlaced her shoes. She rolled her stockings off and tucked them neatly into her shoes. I remembered watching her tuck her stockings under a root before she walked in the creek fifteen years ago. Now she walked over to me, her skirt rippling like a wave. I looked down at my own lap and followed the weave of the calico, as if each knot meant something. Martha touched my shoe. She knelt on the carpet and slipped it off, then she reached up to unclip the top of my stocking. She rolled it down. My leg was shining every place she touched it. I could feel it. Martha unlaced my other shoe. Her hair fell over her face, over my knee, covering the pattern of my skirt. I stroked her head. She lifted my foot into the water.

It was cool. She rubbed her fingertips against my sole, making little circles at the hard places. I had a flicker of embarrassment at my callouses, but then she held my foot between both palms as if it were butter she was trying to press her flower into, and I felt like something precious. Martha washed and rubbed my other foot, then she unbuttoned her white blouse and wrapped it around my feet to dry them. I saw her breasts move against the edges of her corset, then I closed my eyes. Martha dried my feet on the soft cloth. I heard her rise and walk over to the bureau, then she was rubbing my feet with warm oil, slick and tender, rubbing my instep and my ankle, circling the bony knob at the bottom of my calves, both hands rhythmic and steady. I could smell crushed lavendar. Martha slid her fists against the back of my calves, working the knots, then followed with her palms over the back of my knees to the place where my thighs met the chair. She kept one hand on my skin as she raised my skirt to pour more oil on my thighs. I shook a little, as if with a chill. This time she hadn't warmed the oil in her hands.

Martha was on her knees between my legs now, pressing her hands over the tops of my thighs, then pulling them back down the sides. The insides of my knees touched the tight satin over her belly. Every time she leaned forward, her breasts pressed against my undergarments. Now she was resting her hands on her breasts, kneading the damp cotton of my underpants with her thumbs, but not reaching under the cloth. I was pushing against her, crying, not thinking, holding her shoulders, shaking, sliding off the chair with my crotch going over the tips of her breasts, going over her satin belly, slipping down to her thigh where she held me, rocking me back and forth, holding my hips down with both hands as I joined her motion. I was pulsing tighter and tighter when she pushed her finger inside me and rocked me against her thumb. Then I was lost to the senses, lost to description, gone to the milky heart of the world where I churned and churned and churned.

Dimensions

Barbara Herrera

Her touch drives me crazy. I want her fingers on me, in me. I can't get enough of her. Her flesh squishes under my fingers and I squeeze hard enough for her to know I am responding positively to her overtures. Goddess, I love making love with a fat woman! She makes no apologies about the amount of personal space she utilizes or that she likes to sit on two chairs instead of one. I learned early to patronize places that had no arms on their chairs and had bathrooms she could turn around in.

We finally drive into our driveway and I can't get into the apartment soon enough. She presses me up against the wall and surrounds me with her self. "Fuck me, Hill. I want it bad."

We drop the bags of groceries and Hillary undoes the buttons on my jeans. Still leaning against the door, she slides her hand down my belly and into my underwear to touch my wet. She has to wriggle for a moment so she has a good angle, but then she takes one finger and moves it back and forth to spread my lips. I slump over her shoulder, hardly able to contain my grunts and groans. Always wary of the neighbors who insist on banging on the wall in the throes of my passion, I bury my face in her neck.

She takes one finger and pushes it deep into my puss. "Oh, Leya, you are so wet. It's so hot in here."

I feel my clit against her finger and her finger deep inside me. We talked dirty to each other the whole time we were at the store so I am ready to come in her hand. She plunges in and out of me and I begin the early contractions of orgasm. I could have waited longer except her hand is putting so much pressure on my vulva and her finger is rubbing directly on my clit. I sink my teeth into her neck and explode my release of all that anticipation. She holds me tight and lets me shrink into her arms.

I want to make love to her so we put the groceries away and take a candlelit shower together. I love being in here with her. It's so hot and steamy, I always feel like I'm in a movie when I take a shower with someone. Movie sets couldn't be this warm and romantic, though.

She disrobes and stands before me naked and open. I can't see her pubic hair, but I know it is there because I play with it when we are lying in bed. Her hair is sparse because of the ample flesh and I love licking between each of the hairs, tickling her into arousal.

Both of us get into the shower and I watch her lean her head back and get wet. I take the soap and run it down her body, touching, feeling, craving her body. I hold her left breast in my hand and savor the weight of it. Her nipple is the size of the palm of my hand and once again I apologize to her for not being able to please her by taking all of it in my mouth. She looks up, then down, and tells me I please her better than any of her previous lovers. I tell her I bet she says that to all her lovers. She says, "Yes, as a matter of fact, I have said that to all my lovers. I know more about myself and about my body with each lover, so I suppose that is why I say that. Does that make sense?"

I tell her she makes perfect sense and I am so glad she is here to tell me how to please her because she deserves it. She touches the small of my back and pulls me close. "You, too, deserve the best. Tell me where to touch you, my darling Leya."

I turn around and encourage her with the gyrations of my ass. She takes the soap and fills her hands with suds. Bending down, she washes me. Her hands slide around my ass, my puss, cleaning me for later. Her two fingers move up and down with my clit in between them. I feel the heat so acutely now that I'm flushed. The streams of water hit my clit at even intervals. Holding on to the soap dish to avoid falling down, I come once again in her hand.

I sit on the floor to collect myself and ask her to turn the water on cold for a minute. I feel refreshed and turned on by the sudden change in temperature. She laughs as I lunge for her clit and reminds me she can't come standing up. I tell her I don't care and proceed to part her lips so I can go inside her and feel her heat. Oh! The contrast between the cold shower and the heat of her puss is incredible! How does she get so hot? Every time I enter her I am surprised by the intensity of her passion. Even after four years, I shudder each time I squish inside her and make noises in her puddles.

She contracts as I go deep inside her vagina and I lose all of my hand and much of my arm between her thighs. The pressure is intense for both of us as I wiggle my finger around inside her without moving my hand. She loosens up and I put another finger in. I touch what I call her shelf. If I were looking at my hand, my pointer and middle finger would be bent almost to the palm of my hand. That is what I do inside my lover. It drives her crazy. Pressure, release, pressure, release. She moans her pleasure and I see her knees buckling. That is my signal to stop, so I turn the water off and we get out.

I watch her walk to the bed and her body is in motion. Every part of her moves: thighs, breasts, arms, calves, and ass. Oh, he ass! I wish I had enough hands to hold her whole butt at one time. Instead, I ask her to lie down on her stomach so I can massage her. She looks delighted and complies. Her face is buried in the pillows and I squirt lotion on my hands to warm it before rubbing it on her body. Mmmm, I touch the warmed liquid to her dimples and crevices and massage the insides of her thighs. As I touch and honor her, I remember the shock of finding myself crazy in love with a woman well over three hundred pounds.

Some people questioned my motives. "You just want to see what she looks like naked, don't you?"

Some women couldn't believe I really was sexually attracted to her. "Don't you think she should lose weight? She is awfully big."

Still others couldn't imagine what I would do with her when I got to make love to her. "What will you do with all that woman?"

I want to eat her so bad I ask her to turn over. She does and I swoon at her massive breasts lying before me. Quickly I wash my hands so nothing will get into her gorgeous puss. I put my finger in her and lie beside her so I can suck her nipple at the same time.

I always make myself crazy with what to do first, middle, and last. So many places to pleasure her and myself and every time I ask her, she says, "Everywhere." Her nipple is swelling in my mouth and I feel the outer ridges bumping the outside of my lips. She is moaning and moving her hips in rhythm to my fingers while I suck harder and harder, flicking her nipple with my tongue.

She is heavy in her ecstasy and I realize I have yet to eat her. I ask if I can, please, eat her. She slows her hips and tells me, "Eat me now. I want to come in your face."

A shiver of pleasure runs through me and my hand gently leaves her pussy. I prop her up on pillows so she can watch. I love looking up and seeing her face gazing down at me, eyes intense, mouth open and wet. I push her thighs apart and inhale deeply, intoxicating myself with her scent. Her vulval lips are full and swollen. They call me with their own hunger, so I suck on her left lip and slide my tongue on the inside, getting a hint of the juices available so close to my mouth.

I put my hands around her thighs and hold on for the ride ahead. My tongue finds its way into her cavern and I tongue-fuck her and swallow in even intervals of enjoyment. I hold on to her legs as a small orgasm, with a big gush of liquid, tells me it is time to move to her clitoris.

I slide my tongue up and pull my right hand from under her leg at the same time. Her clit has become engorged and I will feed off it until she is spent. My tongue knows the motions, feels where she wants me to lick. My eyes are closed and my face is buried in her puss. My own wet flows unchecked as I eat from my lover and visualize her pleasure. Around and around and around her clit, I move in a design lesbians have known since the beginning of time. Lightly now, I make my breath have more weight than my tongue.

My left hand reaches up and touches her pebble-hard nipple. I wrap my lips around her clit and make my tongue very soft and flat. I figure this will drive her close to orgasm, but I will still have control over when she comes.

My right hand edges up to the opening and relaxes, knowing what comes next. I continue playing with her nipple and licking at her puss, but now I will enter her wet and fuck her as well. I push my finger in tentatively, and with every inward motion, my finger advances farther. When I cannot push in any longer, I pull out a little and add a finger. I repeat the sequence and hear her moan with each advancement. A mantra of "Yes, yes, yes" flows from her lips.

My hands seem small tonight. Perhaps it is her excitement that has made her so open. She is moving her hips to my constant in and out, around and around, pull and tug. Low growls tell me how much pleasure she is feeling and I begin to groan, too. As she nears her climax, her clit gets big in my mouth. Her vagina tightens around my hand, pulling me in, in, in.

I fuck her hard while I suck from her wet. Her body writhes in time to my strokes inside her and my circles around her clit. I feel her arch in expectation. Her vagina contracts around my fingers and I can barely move my hand, so I move my fingers, lick and press from both sides at the same time. This sends her into her last frenzy. She gets still tighter and her clitoris swells until I think it will explode. I have never felt a woman come for as long as she does and it surprises me every time. She continues her pulsations and I stay with her while she is in such a heightened state of enjoyment.

She pushes my head away but lets my hand continue to plunge in and out of her. I feel another orgasm coming on the heels of the one she just had and fuck her hard so she can come again without losing the sensation of the one before. I love hearing her moan to the contractions, her body in perfect synchronization.

She pulls me up to her. I gently remove my hand and revel in her softness. I lay on her side, my head on her heaving chest, my arm around her waist, my leg thrown over hers. "I love you," I say.

When she catches her breath, she says, "I love you, too, baby."

She starts rubbing me absently as she composes herself. I get shivers as I picture her between my thighs, her hot tongue on my warm clit, her fat fingers inside my tight puss, the weight of her body on top of mine as she fucks me hard while I fuck her, and my own orgasm exploding in her face and on her body. Yes, I know what's coming next.

My Buddy

La Verne Gagehabib

I could hear my Buddy calling from her secret place, insisting that only she could ease the pain of desire still present, after my night of love making with my partner. We had satisfied each other time after time. I had been soothed . . . pleased . . . and brought to screaming climax after climax . . . yet . . . I still had a deep ache high in my womanness, that only Buddy could reach, and satisfy. My woman-self throbbed, and fluttered in response to Buddy's summons.

Wait . . . !

Standing on the porch waving, I threw kisses to my departing lover as she drove off in her truck smiling, her face flushed from our night of passion.

Sighing Deeply . . . I waited. Soon, she was out of my sight.

Back in the house I went to get Buddy. Reaching into her hiding place, I groped around, then grasping her firm, solid form. I pulled her out . . . into the open shaking her free from her towel wrap. She was long, black, and flexible. With Buddy clutched firmly in my hand, I headed for the bedroom.

I could feel myself get excited. The pulsating ache between my legs intensified. Grabbing my jugg* pillow I climbed onto the bed. After stripping naked, I inserted Buddy into the pillow and zipped her tight and secure. She stood tall and ready. I leaned forward with my hands pressed against the bed, rubbing my clit against Buddy's firm head.

Ummmmmm . . . ahhhhhhh!

Wiggling my hips I slid down onto Buddy slowly, slipping her deep then deeper into myself. My cunt muscles gripped Buddy in a familiar way, squeezing the phallic, pleasure stick.

Ahhhhhhh.........uh!

In my mind's eye I could see Buddy strapped to my partner, and me on top of her with Buddy deep inside me. Oh course this could not be because, my lover is not into doing Buddy, so I must go on without her. She knows all about me and Buddy, and it's ok in her presence, or alone. I prefer just me and Buddy in our solitude.

Ohhhhhhhhhhhhhhh!

Buddy was thrusting deeper into my womanness, sending ripples of pleasure through out my total being, reaching all the places fingers . . . tongues . . . and hands failed to penetrate. I rode Buddy towards my pleasure, humping her with deep jugging motions.

Haaaaaaaaaaaaaaaaaa! " Oh Baby!"

I began sliding down on Buddy. All the way in . . . to the base, then all way out . . . to the bulbous head, moving my hips so that just the tip touched my clit . . . like a large tongue . . . rubbing up against it.

Shiiiiiiiiii...iiiiiiiii...it!

Reaching down, I pulled Buddy out, bending her head into a crook. Sliding back onto her, she hit just right inside me. My body took over and began moving in a frenzy, like a madwoman on the rubber firmness. I rode Buddy . . . and rode her . . . and rode her!

Yes.......yaaaaaaaaaaaa...yes....y....ye......yes.......YES!

My nature rose higher as my pleasure sought relief, escalating higher.

Aiiiiiiiiiiiiiiiiiii.......ya....................ahhhhhhhhhhh!

I screamed my joy, as I came. My body slumped forward onto the bed, Buddy slipping out of me with a plop.

Uh................hum................!

After some time passed, I rolled off the pillow and onto my hands. Yes, my Buddy had come through for me again. I can always count on my Buddy to be there for me when I need her.

Hummmmmmmmmmmmmm.

I slept.

---

* Jugg pillow is an invention by the author.

What I Will Not Tell You

Lesléa Newman

If you want to hear all the luscious, gory details, forget it. You know I don't talk about those things. I'm just not that kind of girl.

So don't even ask me how I happened to walk into the bar at 11:30 last Saturday night dressed in a red sleeveless mini-dress with a big black belt and three inch heels to match, looking like I was out to get something. Or someone. I'm not gonna tell you. I'm not one to spill the beans.

I'm not even gonna tell you how I spotted her way over at the very end of the bar, or how somehow I could see her plain as day through the dim lights and all that lazy, hazy cigarette smoke that was drifting between us. You can ask all you want, but I have no intention of telling you how I knew she was the one even before the bartender set down a drink in front of me and nodded in her direction.

I will tell you, since you must know, that I did go over and say thank you, and she did answer you're welcome, but I will not tell you any more about our conversation. And I most certainly will not describe her white shirt and how it set off her tan, or her tight jeans that hugged her gorgeous thighs, or her red cowboy boots complete with spurs, because I am sure if I did I'd never hear the end of it.

Since you are so incredibly nosy, I will tell you that yes, we did dance, but even if you beg, I will not divulge what happened when a slow song came on. I will not describe how soft her lips felt as she pressed them hard against mine because they have not yet invented words to describe such a thing. And likewise, since I am not a poet, I couldn't even if I wanted to which I don't, tell you what her arms felt like tight across my back and how her thigh felt sliding itself between my legs and how her breasts felt pressing up against mine underneath her thin cotton shirt.

Even if you begged and pleaded on one knee I couldn't tell you who else was in the bar that night, because frankly, I didn't notice. I can and will tell you that there was no one in the bathroom when I went in to powder my nose, but I won't tell you who knocked on the door a minute after I went in there.

You'll have to guess who came in and stood me gently but firmly against the wall, covering my body with hers and kissing me on the mouth like there was no tomorrow. You'll have to guess who ran her hands up and down my body and whispered oh baby and snuck one of my breasts out the top of my dress and sucked on it like it was a lollipop and she was a kid who never had anything sweet before in her entire life. You'll have to guess who pushed my legs apart and was thankful that I was wearing stockings and a garter belt but nothing else underneath that little red dress. You'll have to guess whose hand reached up and in and whose three fingers I held onto like my life depended on it. You'll have to guess who called me baby doll and told me to give it to her and who thrust her hand in and out faster and harder until I had to bite her neck to keep from screaming. And you can try to figure out just who it was that wiped my cum down the side of her tight jeans and watched me in the mirror with a big grin on her face while I pulled my dress down and combed my hair and put on a fresh coat of lipstick which she promptly kissed right off.

Since I suppose you must get your kicks somewhere, I will tell you that we left the bathroom and went back to the bar and had another drink, but I would never in a million years tell you that I sat on her lap and let her play with me in the dark under my little red dress, and that I sat very prim and proper the whole time while the bartender mopped up a few spills with her soggy towel and chatted to us about this and that. And even if you promised me the moon, which I know you won't, I'm gonna plead the fifth amendment and keep quiet about what happened when another slow song came on and we moved into a corner and locked our thighs and lips together, not caring if everyone and her mother knew what we were doing. No, I will not tell you that we stayed in that dark corner long after the song ended and that her hand snuck itself inside my dress to find my stiff nipples and her knee snuck itself between my legs and took me to a place I'd never been before.

But since you are so very curious, I will tell you that when the bar closed she did walk me out and hail a cab and slip the driver ten dollars to take me home. And she most certainly did open the car door for me and give me a very respectable kiss goodnight.

So don't ask me anymore questions, especially what her name was, because even if you had a fit on the floor I would not tell you even if I knew it which I don't, though I very well might find out when I return to a certain bar at a certain time next Saturday night. Let's just change the subject right now because I am not a kiss and tell type of gal, never was and never will be. If you want to hear that kind of talk, you'll just have to go ask somebody else.

Alexa

Pearl Time'sChild

Given: a stranger appears in your life, a scholar in your own field, here on a research visit. You offer her a place to stay. Now, what is the very best thing you could hope to happen? . . . Be careful what you wish for.

One day, early on

That evening we consumed a lot of alcohol and smoke, came home and built a fire. We stayed up till after two, talking, and beginning to touch and kiss. At some point in the evening I had to bring up the subject of herpes. I *hated* doing that, took a long time to come to saying it.

"You have a Tragic Secret?" she asked, trying to fathom what I needed to tell her. When I finally got it out, she said, "Herpes? What's that?" So I had to explain the whole thing, and talked about my whole history with it. She was very sympathetic; and to my surprise, she did not seem to consider the possibility of getting herpes much of an obstacle. Or she was sure there must be a cure. Or a wrong diagnosis. And she kept touching me, loving me, as we talked. Her hands can be very gentle.

Another day

. . . . Yes, we have made love. Twice, so far. It was Thursday night that years, by now, of celibacy for me were broken. We stayed awake into the wee hours on the couch opened out before the fire. As a result of this debauchery my herpes flared up, so, the next time, I could not let her make love to me. She didn't like that at all.

But *I* could make love to her. And that night I learned that she is a woman who wants to be filled, who wants all my fingers inside her, whose pillowy convolutions welcome me in with powerful convulsions . . . I, also, love, yearn, sometimes to be filled, and nearly pummeled; but I have seldom had lovers who did. However, my tissues are more delicate now since menopause, so delicate, in fact, that I had given up sex even with myself for more than half a year, now, acknowledging the costs too high for such a temporary pleasure, and insignificant, alone.

I like that Alexa is able to articulate what she wants, to say, "I want more of you inside me," and "A little higher. Yes!" and simply "More!" How nice it can be when someone asks.

Another day

I was feeling so open that morning that I made love to her in her bed. At the moment she cannot make love to me, or, rather, my labia are off limits, due to one little red dot I am not sure about. Frustrating. She said the other night it's like being teenagers before contraception. But I don't really mind; I love to be held, kissed, stroked. And even to feel a little unfulfilled desire is a nice state for me. I am a patient person. And, anyway, I have had plenty of orgasms in my life. And, surprisingly, I find there is a tinge of the stone butch in me in this relationship, of not being entirely ready to yield to her my vulnerability, to give her the power to make me quake and whimper and give myself up to my longings past all disguises.

As things are now, if I never see her again after next Tuesday, I will thank the universe for a pleasant, loving, and instructive interlude, and eagerly turn back to the rest of my life, hopefully enriched and stimulated by the experience. . . . Not that my being brought to orgasm by a woman means I couldn't let go of her, or hold her lightly in my life. . . . No, it's in the act itself. In my not easily feeling the trust needed to be naturally that open.

Another day

Snow falling. Yesterday I performed my writing and songs at my "Faculty Lecture." Afterwards we went out for lunch, and spent the afternoon running errands. It was all very pleasant and fun. And when we got home she fixed me a simple shrimp dinner with champagne. "For the weary Frau Professor after her big lecture," she said.

It was very nice to put my feet up before the fire and eat, and watch her give the cats their new toys. Afterwards I lay with my head in her lap, and she stroked me, and I stroked whichever cat was in my lap at the time. And after that she stroked me long, until, almost before I realized it, she was making love to me, and was reaching inside, and bringing up moisture, and stroking my clitoris in a wonderfully pleasurable way, though I could have told her that does not bring me to orgasm. Except that there did come a point where I found myself in the grip of that river of pleasure and excitement and single-focused need. And then there did come a point where I gave up my last defenses, and came, in an orgy of needing and having, needing and having.

Afterwards, we slept together in my bed, expressing love for each other, and gladness that this was not the last night we would be together (as per her original plans to fly home this morning, changed only yesterday). Half way through the night I woke with a tickle in my throat; she transferred to her own bed, and I made again my nest of pillows.

Another day, much later, after she had left

Was Alexa right? Do I prefer money-grubbing over the glories of love? . . . After a certain point, yes.

"You know, class really is a factor here." I said, one evening toward the end.

"Oh, intellectuals are classless," she protested.

"There may be truth in that," I said. "But some intellectuals have more leisure and money than others. I *have* work I have to do to hold my life together."

"*I* work, too," she said. "But I somehow manage to do it when other people aren't around. I *always* have time for my friends. I don't know, different values I guess. *I* work, but I don't get in people's faces about it."

"The only reason you even know about my work is because you're living in my house!" I protested, incredulous. I had come home late from a meeting, after a very hard day, the fifth, of building fence at my rental house. My body, unused to physical exertion after a recent injury, was learning again what it is to move, and have energy and strength; but by suppertime I was very tired. And I had to get up early tomorrow to finish the job.

"You're *living* in my house, driving *my* car every day, and you're *upset* because I'm not paying you more attention?" "But Pearl! Our time is so short! There are so many wonderful things we could be doing! That seems not to matter to you!"

Often before my defenses were caught up with the realization, "This woman *loves* me!" . . . But not this time.

"I could move away to a hotel," she said. "But then I'd *never* see you. I'd rather stay here and fight with you than that."

"Did it ever occur to you to wonder," I thought, but did not say, " what I would prefer?"

On the morning she left, we sipped Riesling in the airport restaurant. Her plane had been called to board, but she was ignoring it until the last moment. She was in the mood for summations, the good and the bad.

We had just had a nice time together as I drove us, with a side trip to the ocean, to the city where she would catch the plane. I'd enjoyed showing her my favorite beach. The tide was the lowest I've ever seen; a full moon coinciding with a particularly close perihelion. We saw lots of anemone, and studded starfish. "Sea stars," she told me they are called in the languages of Europe. But when she pulled a mussel or limpet or whatever it was from a rock and exclaimed in excited interest, "Look! It bleeds!" I could not help but feel a little horrified. All the Same, I ate seafood afterwards, and acknowledged that both it and the wine were delicious.

She bought a second bottle to have in the motel later: but I drove there slowly, because of the dark, and the winding road, and the wine I'd had. And, even more, to make it be too late by the time we got there, so that I would not have to make clear to her my new determination not to further mix our body fluids. She seemed to sense it anyway, and did not press the point.

There was one bed in the room; and we shared it comfortably, even affectionately.

There had been something nice about being able to reach out and touch hands, touch bodies, comfortably, attractedly.

And it had been nice to be so clearly lesbian in public, in all those restaurants she'd taken me to in those past weeks. Even while I sometimes thought, "*She* doesn't have to go on living here. *I* do." But mostly it was nice not to worry if our hands touched, held, even caressed, or played with each other absently as we talked and ate.

Now, in the airport restaurant, we let our hands touch again. We had spent the morning talking about her novel; it had been good to remember some of the reasons we had for connecting. It is not so usual for her, either, to know another woman in her field, who is also a lesbian, and a writer. I'm sure I am special to her.

She said, "Maybe it's good we spent this much time together. Now we know both sides."

I did not say it was a too-expensive lesson, or that I had seen "both sides" coming early on.

Now, for all the goodness of holding hands, and being at the end of an intense experience with someone, I was clear about my reservations. "For example, the way you were that night, about the fence, " I said, "that was just not acceptable."

"But how about the next night?" she smiled. "When we ended up at the French restaurant, and I showed you Irish creme? Was *that* acceptable?"

It *had* been pleasurable, rolling the liqueur around on my tongue as she instructed, holding it in my mouth, attending to the series of delicious changes it underwent as it heated, mixed with the juices of my mouth, explored the regions of my tongue.

"Yes," I answered her, smiling too. She was leaving in ten minutes; what was the use? "Yes, I don't deny there have been many enjoyable times, and that there were reasons we got together."

I saw her through the check-in gate, and even felt a little

poignant as she disappeared up the escalator. As I turned to leave, I noticed the security guard who had witnessed our goodby. With short-cut hair, and a capable manner of sitting, she was looking at me with what surely seemed to be an expression of sympathy. We shared a tiny smile of recognition.

I walked to the parking lot, and sat in my car, collecting my feelings. . . . A touch of sadness. . . . And the first little waves of relief.

"Still," I thought, finishing our last conversation, "an unacceptable and an acceptable – don't add up to an acceptable.

fire of my heart

H. Zednik

(dedicated to dt)

december

now let the remembering begin.

time of slow delicious tasting and recalling easing down to examine fully feel force and beauty of past weeks months days then from that build and rekindle fire again and again.

glowing becomes waiting to be with you.

my heart this cavern your hand pushed to open now i hear faint rustling echo of where you stretched your wings and told you loved me.

today winter solstice we talked from foreign countries of our passion lust.
missing is not adequate.
longing does not describe.

through the snow storm i walked to the graveyard red candles covered the hill and i was touching you back home we'd placed white candles throughout the house as we often did i met you next to the table you still wore your work clothes pulling close past into one i ran my hands down your back.

you are strength to me.
you leaned against the dresser when i slipped my hand into your pants we were both wet i felt you kissing not my mouth but my body while your tongue never left my lips.

i am passion explosion images words for you and us.

i licked curry paste off your fingers lovingly passed a piece of chocolate back and forth wine i have been fed from your lips clementines bit in half juice running down our chins i know the sound of the pomegranate being pulled open translucent burgundy collecting between your breasts i hid a seed in your belly button then slowly ate it out.

when i brought you a glass of wine in the shower you invited me we were already late for dinner my clothes wet from leaning against you kissing i threw my clothes on the rug then hot water all over me i pressed your arms away out up the shower wall *i have dreamed of this a long time now.* water ran in our mouths our moving bodies made sucking sounds.

ready to come you are edge contentment insanity ecstasy the quivering holding almost over you sometimes throw the pillow over your face put your arm over your eyes.
you are vulnerable then.

i love you.

another time in the bathroom i roamed all over you one foot on the toilet leaning against the sink for balance those were often desperate times we knew we had one month so we lived and love -fucked a life full. i have never desired anyone so much your word my body rises your gesture i feel fire.

i my body never wants to find your end.

the tenderness as passionate as the sex our living together a practice of love making.

you are with me all the time here even now i wear the green robe the one you said would make love to me i can smell you and myself woven into this fabric i have loved you in this robe you have covered me with this robe when we lay naked i now sleep with this robe cocooning it around me.
i know it is not you.

my hands know the fill of your breasts my tongue traces in memory the expanse and shift of your nipples i have spent hours painting this on ricepaper thin as skin my brush moist on paper parchedness nothing like the first time i lay next to you softness cascading into lushness.

i do not want these words to become lamentations of distance and separation.

it is you i desire these words to be.

your body the heavens skin stars stretching over around me you whisper wind breast hills rise to me i am home in your caverns where i have found ripple images and buried myself this giving me infinite comfort to survive because we do often have to defend.

hours i can kiss drawing breath from your lips.

the snow has returned to rain rivers will now roar through these mountains part of me torn and rushing with them for all water ends in ocean and i then closer to you.

during dreams i visit you nightwings being merely a question of expanding a moment.

between dark blue grey mountains sun set your body cradled in mine we'd been up alpine meadow with cold wind i will never forget the late night glowed warm burning behind you.
fire eyes you are life to me.
simple to recognize the gift we are to each other.
going down i ran free through tall calico grass the wind had combed it flat we found a cup of warm earth to lie down in.

next to each other we are outside time.

at dusk i collected red lanterns for you fire of my heart.
i understand the need now the desire to unpeel you i said digging for skin naked honesty to feel breasts and bones.

dried ginger and chili peppers i have found hands hot with spice.
this is no substitute for you.
i kiss your lips nibble nectar sweet passion burns for you here when will you be near?

my hands smeared with paint i have been at your body drawing lines trying to find you i walk through villages seeing for you down rain wet streets skipping icy cobblestones rhythms of love i want to kiss you in churches bright blue purple stained glass drum yap howl for you.

tomorrow i go to vienna city of my father will i find laughter among buildings grey monuments of decadence i smoke in anticipation my addictions soar red velvet lust i will tell of our love i will sing our love to prancing horses and statues i wish i might have built for you.

christmas eve i love you.
thoughts scattered thousands of miles pushed between us i feel you near but want you bodily to curl against tasting smooth to worked surfaces of skin kissing you slowly o so slowly from toe to nipple to ear then tangle our tongues NOW i want to be with you NOW.

the snow reckless tumbling to gentleness night tender new whiteness and i longing to share warmth next to you then slowly drift to dream.

the flakes now thicker twisting dancing curtain hangs between me and lake mountains secret in clouds not so different from the lace in our bedroom some mornings sun fingered through splinter gaps stretching to warm your face here i have not seen the sun twelve days.

you i believe fire to be.

i recall how easily we shared love into others they saw our passion belief and came for more drawn to fire giving.

early night morning conversation our trans-atlantic reading my mouth dry with wanting and all i could give these words.

i have often kissed parting curls soft and salty hand on chest lapping lipping exalting desire rhythms your legs pushed out strong the accident's trace memory to thank thank thank your being for me now to give myself in pleasing down.

with strength i sometimes want you pushing hard it becomes a screaming when the heart can hold no more.

our beginning in words and letters your voice touching me Asheville to Chicago often then i questioned emotions abstract undefinable now i never doubt love strong strong fierce rooting deep we are one i dream to grow old trace age lines over your body and mine.

here the trees old naked standing winter grey the wind a force ragging ripping ice i find heat in recalling you melting you keep me real i fear distance freezing but trust the speed of traveling fire.

from you i ask flames to torch my winter.

these words begin to hold the future i speak events unlived in sounding these lines i bring you near loud each vocal roll and roar.

gingerheart let me curry you facedown my body stretching your back breasts of mine meet strong shoulders oil to slip along spine to opening caves from behind will you come when fingers push inside believing this i slowly begin to drip for my hands know the opaque treasures they will find.

the sadness eases excitement rises in believing i will cross continents to you vision fantasies of unbuttoning pulling off frenzy o free your skin of color soft clothes rearrange the house with traveling bodies rugs bed walls halls kitchen bath chairs let nothing separate us.

in London dimmer comprehension of this mad dash twenty four hour decision to see you no doubt sanest action i've ever committed somewhere over Canada i begin to smile my body simmering anticipation holding you in two hours with ten days to go my belly sings yes yes my heart scream hums loud glory thanks.

january

again apart you called from Florida spoke sun and warmth how little you wore while i laughed snow and wear all your voice sounding free i asked of freckle explosions saying how i would like to count intimate skin galaxy linger days discovering down where they disappear to cavern lips moist seashell warm.

alone now mornings my first thoughts of you body missing lover fire i race down stairs to stoke wood stoves release geese heat water for coffee never once letting you far from my heart i look out the window see snow quietly settling mountains soaring i will try to remain happy in this two hundred and sixty two year old house where i dream our bodies steam stone walls and windows.

i need you to speak with me the missing days our privacy would we be telling those ten days when i flew to meet you no record or written words only black and white pictures of carved angels two of us arms wrapped round everyone asks to know those times how do you say i cannot even begin to tell?

it is those images i have of you now when we walked the cemetery daily homage to angels strong winged women each time our bodies closer merging stopping every few steps to laugh kiss tongue waltz and whisper slow *i love you i love you.*

open i feel to intertwine my fingers in yours warm my body surrounds i want to be with you mornings midnights wake you in sleep find you darkness soft buttocks breasts clit curves to lip dance and wonder am i dreaming your loving or are we night real?

our bodies sweat wet close dream traveling we smile dawn to sex love relaxed our orgasms crash and roll then share hot coffee steamed sweet milk while i read out loud erotic short stories till noon or longer then begin again.

snow falling dusk i walked into St. Peter's cathedral empty except for organ music humming the walls up up and up votive candles burned a thousand red cups shimmering sea flickering with cold wind which always circles through such places i lit a candle for you placed it in waves of bright white heat then into these flames gently spoke your name love thanks.

i woke with you waltzing my heart white turned early morning rose i stayed in bed to dream you come spring i will pick first snow roses with you walk across soft stretch thawing earth and love you thousand fold for every petal opening sun.

beauty aches these days: mirror of your absence.

close i desperately recall every surface movement smell of you want to feel brushing warmth of whispered words i desire you.

this morning vine creeps up bones from feet ungrounded to thorn twist round my heart firework crack blast my brain with memories of touch-laugh-hold and kiss.

what warm wind caresses you this dawn?

to the frozen pond i went to throw wild energy love explosion i'd been talking to you south glowing ember i spread my arms to blue sky pushing clouds and snow wind circled round me dog and i howled whiteness whiteness why do you keep me here?

deliberate music we played catapulting us raw teasing passion wild dancing ourselves naked pushing against walls one traveling up the other down cold wood floor met sweat wet skin our bodies' rhythms changing with each song.

smooth thighs meet moisture glory moisture dance with me dance with me skin to skin swing and sway soft hips tingle nipples hard of rose let this be our private rock to midnight waltz.

breathless after ninety minute nonstop lust and sex exact duration of maniac tape marathon quiet on the floor with wonder and exhaustion nothing inhibiting with you i will try the world inside out.

when i see you next will i first kiss you madly airport public hold you fifteen minute tight hug stop moving bodies traffic attempting to bridge long physical separation in seconds or silently take your hand smile lean close to gently whisper warm i want to love you will the car be our first haven rediscover smoldering presence we are to each other perhaps the train to take us blur of foreign passing cities farms and fields we could close the curtains jam the door ignite first spring fires.

last night's dream left lust vein crackling heart beating tumbled memories of first sight attraction remembering this woman i would like to wake to i open eyes see air around me fire.

in Graz i lay wild wanting nolonger can i remember you physically escape description but tongue tingles tastes of you.

february

first day of February i allow myself to count leap year days your arrival still unknown i will not let my heart hold time precious but finally i am one month's word closer to you.

three fifteen your call burst the afternoon march third march third came the words i could barely breath thirty two days the distance stands.

a compass you sent me that i might not lose my way or drift unawares aren't we both seeking new paths want health and sanity see in each other knowledge support and spiritual balance for all this i love you more.

when you called last night friend and i (in contradiction to truth seeking) had already laughed and read our way through most a bottle of vodka i wanted to hold you on the phone for hours but now next morning am left knowing little of your current life except on an island when it rained you wanted to make love to me and i the same that you spent hours fun picking lingerie you valentine shipped which i now wear crack teasing dreaming on.

will you oil me suck me fuck me let me lap smell sweet salt of lover cream send fire racing legs and spine kiss me never ending lips twist round nipples stiff tease my clit finger hand till i can come no more.

then please o please begin again.

for then i will oil you fuck and suck make you sweat push you arch to bend edge ecstasy later we'll lie wet tangled sheets love laugh o hum soft bliss.

missing your calls spit rips my heart irritation in return i cannot find you no number to reach you having no house but home to van drive sleep anywhere you may wander leave no maps not that i seek destination but please don't say you'll call tomorrow it leaves me hang hoping.

i imagine your body salty brown and beautiful sun warmed no lines interrupt limbs smooth strong musky beach smell of lover's key your island sanctuary.

your words come letters and cards sweet jewels they are i greedily inhale then later read and reread savoring over days we write this intimacy to send.

masturbating last night cold room and covers warm suddenly sand under me expanse o horizon wide open i flew with you water dark and stars uncountable ocean roar pushing me melt to earth remember remember flesh from clay and fire burn it was for you i came lover of flames.

separated i fell in love with you second apart i nearly went insane flew back from Austria to kiss and hold you in your continent now count three i see the strength we gain each day my love more explodes and grows vines out my hands and eyes to reach all around but i know yes certain i do not want this distance anymore.

sunday Salzburg the birds are announcing spring screaming burst this soil soft sod i here in bed under foreign covers miss you more each day closer thoughts intense i cannot think of anything else except you you you crash and roll through body brain lips and toes i remind myself to breath we have nine days yet to go.

dusk is now a warm comfort glow spring earth this is winter's end you sent me sea petals translucent shells of orange and white they brought me ocean laughter roar.

march

two days now the distance crawling crawling i can barely stand this waiting these sixty four days of lost nearness have left me exhausted numb from missing and wanting the intensity and near insanity of this separation behind me brushfire burned black and hollow i wonder have we become foreign to one another and i fear a little will we need to begin our knowing again?

hours away you presently fly ocean unspeakable gift to me i shiver shaking leaf from belly comes earthquake quiver force i want i wait count million minutes o please please come near.

aimlessly i bump hour to hour i am barely here so close so close you are to complete fire raging i can feel beauty bursting skin tomorrow love will torch my spring and all will be all will be.

you are here with me now.

Courting Pleasure

Tee A. Corinne

Laughter isn't the first thing some people think about when they think about sex, but for me it's part of the whole package. That was the first thing I noticed about her, her big laugh and the comfortable way she wore her clothes. Later, when we had become lovers, that laugh or even one of her generous chuckles would get me all excited, remembering. But that's getting ahead of my story.

I grew up back east and came here with my husband. Then he dumped me. I was forty-four and all I'd ever done was raise children and flowers and keep the house spotless, the way he liked it. The children were off doing their own thing, as they say, and he did his with a woman not much older than they.

I was in shock for awhile, then someone steered me into a displaced homemakers program at the local community college. They called me a re-entry woman, taught me how to write a resume and brushed up my typing and filing skills. A year later I was typing and filing for the college at a little over minimum wage.

I made one close friend during the year, along with a lot of good acquaintances. My friend, Jed, is gay. His lover left him the same month my husband left me and we cried on each other's shoulder a lot. He was having supper with me when he asked, "How'd you like to go to a rodeo?"

I'd never been to one, but I was game.

"It's gay," he said.

"I've never heard of a gay rodeo."

"It's a lot like the other kind."

"Sure," I said, pretty sure at least, that I wanted to go.

I kept thinking about the rodeo all week, worried a bit that I'd feel out of place. Thursday I left work early and went to a western clothing store where I spent some of my vacation money. This was, after all, a two day vacation.

The sunshine was hot, but the breeze kept us cool. There were people all over the place. Some of the men were prettier than I'd ever been, but most looked like the men I meet on the street every day. Then I heard her laugh. It was a big laugh and I turned around to see where it came from. She was holding the reins of a large spotted horse, leaning back and laughing at the sun. A couple of men and a woman were standing there, too, big grins on all their faces.

"Who's she?" I asked Jed.

"Don't know," he said, "but that sure is a pretty horse."

We found a place to sit near the railing and I was watching when she came out riding that big, spotted horse. It was bucking like it was no longer her friend and she was hanging on and hollering and waving her hat in the air. I'd never seen a woman act like that, not even the other women riders.

I though surely she'd be thrown, but no, she stayed on the whole time then jumped off and someone did something to make the horse stop bucking. She and the horse put their faces together like they were the best of friends and she hugged it.

As she started out of the arena she saw me watching and tipped her hat.

"Well," said Jed, "that didn't take you long."

"What didn't?" I asked, but I thought I knew what he meant.

About the time the calf roping started, I felt a hand on my elbow.

"My name's Parker," she said, "and I'd like to get to know you."

"I'm Ronnie and I'm not gay." It just came out of me like that. I felt so foolish.

She laughed like the first time I saw her then grinned at me and asked if I wanted to come see her horse. Jed said yes for me and gave me a gentle shove.

We pushed our way out of the crowd and I stopped to get a soda and to slow things down a bit.

"What do you do when you're not here, showing off?" I asked, noticing that the Coke was especially good.

"I break horses," she said, leaning against the side of the concession stand and looking at me with a grin. "Break horses and train horses and board horses about a hundred miles east of here."

"That's pretty isolated country," I said, imagining an area map.

"Isolated, dry, dusty, lonely and lovely," she said, pushing her hat back a bit and wiping the back of her hand across her forehead. "Want to come visit?"

I thought I should have taken time to consider it, but "Yes" is what I said, then tried to take it back a little. "Yes, I think so. Wouldn't it be an imposition."

"No way," she said, and the grin was bright.

We looked at her horse and then another she was thinking of buying. Now and then she put her hand under my elbow to show me what direction to go, but it was all very proper even though my mind was spinning.

"Are you sure you don't mind that I'm not, you know, a lesbian?"

"I don't mind. I'm just not paying it much attention," she said, directing me away from a pile of horse manure. "Do you ride?"

"Horses?"

"Anything."

"Some neighbors of my grandparents had a pony they let me ride as a kid. I haven't been on one for almost forty years."

"It'll come back."

"Why?"

"That's what you do when you visit me. Ride horses."

"I see," I said, but I wasn't very sure.

I spent some more of my vacation money that week making sure my car was in good shape. I hadn't been anywhere but to the rodeo for a long, long time. I thought I should be worrying or at least wondering what I was getting myself into, but I just felt happy, like I had a very special friend.

Wednesday Anna, my baby, called to tell me I was going to be a grandmother in about six months and that she and David had gotten married so all the paperwork would be in order. I was delighted about the baby, although I still have my reservations about David. He doesn't seem like the staying kind to me, but it's none of my business, really, and she likes him a lot.

Denny, my daughter-in-law called Thursday. Rob, my oldest just went into an alcohol and drug treatment program. She said she was going to leave him if he didn't.

You know, you go along living your life as best you can and raising your children and one day you look back and wonder what you could have done different. I wonder that, but I don't know. I want them to be happy and sometimes they are.

I started early Saturday for Parker's ranch. The mountains all around were jagged and I knew I was alone out there in those open spaces, but I didn't feel lonely. I could see so far. It was a powerful feeling.

There wasn't anything like that where I grew up. The mountains were small by comparison and we lived in town, near Dad's work. I guess it wasn't a town, really. It was a small city, but nothing like the big cities I've seen since then. We had a friendly neighborhood.

Wish Mom and Dad had lived to see the great-grandbabies.

The sign said "Parker's Ranch" in big, cut out letters with fancy designs on either side. I drove under it and another two miles to her house and stables.

I sat in the driveway for a while, looking around. The buildings were weathered gray, but everything was neat and orderly. I went and knocked on the door, but no one answered so I wandered around toward the stables, and then I heard her laugh.

It tickled me and made me want to laugh along with her, without even knowing what she was laughing about.

"Parker," I called when the laughter died away. She put her head out a window, waved and told me she'd be right out.

"Did it take you long to get here? My, don't you look nice!" She leaned over and sniffed my neck. "Smell nice, too."

I laughed. "It took three hours and I wouldn't mind something cold."

"Done," she said and took my arm, steering me back toward the house. "After we get you fixed up we can ride out to look things over and you can decide if you want to stay. Lunch is packed and the horses are saddled."

"Stay?"

"Yeah, or come back. A lot."

"Oh," I said because I really didn't know what to say.

She made me put sun shade on before we went out and said she would lead the horse if I was scared, but I was ready for that horse and rode, pretending it was the old pony, pretending I knew what I was doing, and after awhile it felt like I did.

"Did you grow up around here?" I asked when we paused, side by side to look out over a gray-green field.

"Right here," she said. "First time I was thrown was at the other end of this field. First woman ever left me said goodby under those pines."

"Have there been many women?"

"Some," she said, "and some lulus, too," and then she laughed and turned her horse away. "Come on, now. Let's eat by the creek up ahead."

I followed her, wondering about the lulus. Would I be another?

After lunch I napped on the blanket. When I woke she was gone, but both horses were still there. I walked along the stream and found her sitting on a log, looking out over the grassland. I sat down beside her, but didn't say anything, just looked around at the space, a bird circling slowly in the wide bright sky.

Riding back she encouraged me to go faster.

"I don't like bouncing around," I said, worrying about how sore I was going to be.

"There's a trick to it," she said. "If you trot, you bounce. Go faster and the horse's gate smooths out. Squeeze with your knees and hold on."

She made a clicking sound to her horse and took off. Mine followed without me doing anything. I squeezed my legs to the horse's sides and leaned forward, hooking my hands around the saddle horn. She was right about the ride smoothing out. I felt myself coming alive out there in all that open space. I could feel and match the horse's movements. The wind pushed against me and I breathed it in.

And then Parker's horse slowed up ahead of me and mine did too. I bounced a few times in the saddle before the horse began to walk.

"We'll be able to see the house in a few minutes. It's a good idea to walk them all the way back."

"Fine with me," I said, catching my breath, feeling light-headed from the excitement of the ride, and may more. I didn't think ahead to what would happen later, tonight, tomorrow.

At the stable Parker tied the horses and I slid into her arms. I thought she might kiss me, but surprised myself by kissing her first. Such softness and salt and the horses nickering and nudging us.

She showed me how to take off the saddle and then the bridle and put them away. And then she took my hand and we walked out of the coral and over to the house.

"Do you want a shower?" she asked, raising one eyebrow in a quizzical way, "or a hot tub?"

"Hot tub?"

"It may be wild out here, but I like my amenities."

"I think I'll take a shower." I was out there on the edge of daring already. A hot tub might send me over the edge.

"Take as long as you like," she said, leaving me with a huge fluffy towel.

The bathroom was oddly tiled in a dull-surfaced brown, rustic, yet elegant. Parker was like that, too. I liked her a lot, more than I would have believed possible. It felt so comfortable here. Must be a lot of work, though. But I wasn't afraid of work. What was I doing? I hardly knew the woman and I wasn't gay, was I. Surely I would have known before this.

A plant bloomed in the window. I soaked instead of showering, stretching out my legs and wondering how they'd feel later.

When I came out, wrapped in the towel, Parker was washed and dressed in clean jeans and a bright shirt, leaning against the wall, looking out. I decided I couldn't wait around until evening, anticipation would exhaust me. I walked over to her and unsnapped her shirt, one snap at a time.

She watched me, a slight smile playing at the corners of her mouth.

"You're sure?" she asked, leaving me alone, just watching.

"Yes," I answered, and I was. I unbuckled her belt and unzipped her pants, but had to have her help to get them off. I was glad she'd left her boots off when she'd washed. They would have really slowed me down.

"The bed? The couch, The floor?" she asked as I paused, just looking at her. Her face and neck and hands were much darker than the rest of her, dark as her nipples, but not as dark as her pubic hair. I couldn't think of what to say and just went on looking at her body, at the muscles and curves and soft places.

"Come to bed," she said, gently taking my hand and leading me into another room. She unfastened the towel, let it drop and lay down on top to the bedcovers. It was a big bed, much bigger than I would have thought she'd have.

She lay there with her hands behind her head and let me look some more. The room was warm, but some of the heat was probably coming from inside of me. I moved in slow motion to the foot of the bed, then crawled the length of her, looking and touching. She left me alone, understanding that this was something I had to do.

When I reached her chest I kissed her and slid my body down against her. She reached around me then and held me soft and tight and we kissed for a very long time. I wasn't sure what to do next, but she moved under me and I understood how to move back against her, like learning to move as one with the horse.

We were riding then, each move matched by the other's, breath coming in gasps, the room and bedding immaterial as we rode and rode and then I came, we came together.

I was out of breath and drenched with sweat. Her shoulder tasted salty. Her neck tasted salty. I kissed her lips and cheeks and eyes and eyebrows and hairline and ears.

I really got into her ear, closing my eyes and feeling it with my tongue. She chuckled and hummed and I could tell she really liked it so I continued. Then I moved down her neck and across her chest, licking and kissing until I came to her breast. I took her nipple into my mouth and she drew her breath in sharply. I held the other one in my fingers and squeezed and she drew in another breath and let out a little moan. I could feel her hands moving over my back and in my hair and the room had cooled down a bit, but not much.

Sucking on her breasts reminded me of when my children were babies and how much I had enjoyed nursing them. This, though, was comforting and exciting at the same time. I felt a little braver and started working my way down and past her belly, moving slowly, always ready to stop or turn back if I got scared.

But it wasn't scary. Her pubic hair was soft and I parted it, looking. I knew what I looked like, but had never seen another woman except when I helped with a birth one time and the baby was already starting to crown when I got there.

Parker's sex was pretty, like a small animal in a nest. I parted the lips and traced their shape, like a leaf, like a shell. I wondered if I would know what to do, if I could do it right, but I knew what it felt like to be made love to this way, knew what my own body responded to. I leaned down, closed my eyes and touched her with my tongue. More salt and that lovely odor that I used to notice after he made love to me. I'd never realized where it came from.

I licked and touched, licked and touched and she said, "Yes," and, "Yes," and moaned and I could tell she was excited by what was happening. I could feel my own body responding with hers and I realized she could touch me, too, if I moved around and I did.

How long did we go on like that? I have no idea. I was swimming in pleasure, surrounded by comfort and feelings, sensations the likes of which I had never known. When I came this time, when we both came, it was an explosion, turbulent waters rocking us and lifting us, lifting us and swaying us and then slowly letting us down.

We didn't talk for a long time. The sun went down. She pulled a blanket over us.

"Well," I said, "maybe I am a little bit that way, you know, gay."

"Maybe," she said and held me tight and laughed and laughed.

CONTRIBUTORS' NOTES

Sally Bellerose I was born on July 24, 1951 in Holyoke, Ma. and am a nurse and mother who loves to dance. My work has appeared in numerous journals and anthologies including *Sinister Wisdom, The Sun, The Poetry of Sex,* and *The Persistent Desire.*

I write about sex because it's a complicated part of the human experience. Writing is one way of exploring and understanding. I write about sex for the pleasure of it.

Toni Brown I am an African-American Lesbian, writer of poetry and short fiction. My work has been published in *Sinister Wisdom, Common Lives/Lesbian Lives, The Poetry of Sex: Lesbians Write the Erotic,* and *Tuesday Night,* a chapbook by the Valley Lesbian Writing Group.

I live in Western Massachusetts and am a 40 year old Scorpio. I was born in Boston, Massachusetts, November 4th, 1952. I grew up in a small steel mill town in Pennsylvania. My father was in the navy, then worked in the steel mill. I am the first person in my mother's family to go to college. I graduated from the University of Massachusetts with a B.S. in psychology. I am the mother of a grown son. I have always wanted to write and have written to save my own life. I have never formally studied the craft of writing. (To "waste" a college education in the English department learning to write was ridiculed and dismissed as something black girls just did not do.) I have always wanted to study with a writer sharing ideas and feedback. That is not something that I have been able to accomplish. I do what I feel is the next best thing, I read as much as I can of the work of authors I admire: Toni Morrison, Toni Cade Bambara, Alice Walker, Etheridge Knight, Ntozake Shange, Sharon Olds, Pat Parker, Audre Lorde, Kate Rushin, Becky Birtha, Julie Blackwomon and most recently I have been devouring the work of Lucille Clifton.

I love writing erotic stories and poetry. It is not only fun, but it allows me to express all the sensual ways a lesbian woman can be that I can imagine. It is important for lesbians to have access to erotic writing by lesbians. There is a difference in the way the words feel in the mouth when they have come from one who knows and loves lesbians. All sex writing is not pornography. Any Lesbian offered a variety of erotic choices can decide what touches her woman lovin' heart, what makes her hot.

Coleen Carmen (born December 1, 1956) is a 36 year old Lesbian and native San Franciscan who dreams of living other places. She wants to find a rural/academic locale yet wonders if she will have to trade the crowded freeways for small-town homophobia. "Second Wind" started writing itself in 1986 and is Coleen's first published short story. Lesbian Erotic Fiction challenges the writer/reader to expose the secrets of her own experience. Sex is primal and expansive. It is also paradoxically the most **removed** from written language. Sharing our erotica validates the familiar memories of our bodies; the cherished wisdom discoverable about our lives and each other.

Tee A. Corinne Born Nov. 3, 1943 in St. Petersburg, Florida, into a family of Welsh, English, Scottish, Dutch and French descent, I dreamed and drew my way through a childhood wilderness, never imagining that I would grow up to write. After a masters degree in art and 7½ years of marriage I started working for San Francisco Sex Information Switchboard where talking about sex was a mission. *The Cunt Coloring Book* (1975) grew out of my involvement with the wild and inclusive S.F. sex education community, a group whose influence can also be seen in the books I have written: *Dreams Of The Woman Who Loved Sex, Lovers, The Sparkling Lavender Dust Of Lust*; and those I have edited: *Intricate Passions, Riding Desire*, and *The Poetry Of Sex: Lesbians Write The Erotic.*

doris davenport: born Jan. 29, 1949 in Gainesville, GA. Ph. D. (literature) from USC in 1985. Self-published three books of poetry. Has received writing grants from the Kentucky Foundation for Women, the North Carolina Arts Council, the Syvenna Foundation, and the Georgia Council for the Arts. Recently finished book of communal-autobiographical poetry, *Soquee Street.* Presently struggling to live as a freelance writer (and recovering alcoholic) in my beloved Cornelia, GA.

For me, erotic/sex writing by wimmin is – when it's done well – a necessary *voyage* into another realm, one that is ever-present but not consciously. Not often enough. If i'm doing it, eroticism, sex, and writings about it must also incorporate the provocatively elusive, and always, a sense of humor and playfulness!

Jyl Lynn Felman is an award winning short story writer. Her stories, prose and review essays can be found in many journals and anthologies including: *The Tribe Of Dina, Word Of Mouth, Speaking For*

Ourselves, A Loving Voice, Tikkun, Bridges, The National Women's Studies Journal and *Gay Community News*. She received an MFA in Fiction at the University of Massachusetts in Amherst, and was awarded a Writing Fellowship. She is also a lawyer and lectures throughout the U.S. on Anti-Semitism, Racism and Homophobia. Aunt Lute Books published her first collection of short fiction *Hot Chicken Wings* which was a 1993 Lambda Literary Finalist.

She writes, "I long to feel homoerotic desire reflected back to me. Writing about sex makes desire in my own tongue visible. I see my wanting from my point of view: a Jew and a lesbian. I name my erotic for myself while also naming how I am objectified. Sex writing (by other lesbians and gay men of all classes and colors) allows me to read the body: if it's good – hot – it makes me wet and hungry; if it's bad or offensive, I am called to respond. Lesbian sex writing is necessity; a contradiction to the narrow, rigid heterosexual images that are everywhere. Without lesboerotic writings/photographs, I am left to imagine myself whole; to create my own sexuality without audience, viewer or participant. Sex writing insists on the erotic; I thrive on that insistence."

Ayofemi Folayan I have been fortunate to journey through several careers: musician, actor, paralegal investigator, substance abuse counselor, communications software engineer, and writer/teacher of creative writing. I am grateful that my life has led me to work that I love and which sustains me on all levels. I have lived in California for twenty years, and I am still trying to remember why I moved here. The greatest joy of my life has been the birth of my granddaughter Mawiyah, and watching her grow gives me intense pleasure. Because I struggle with physical disabilities and survived severe childhood traumas, I use creativity as a tool for healing physical, emotional and spiritual wounds. I have healed myself by communicating the pain of racism, incest, physical abuse, and neglect in a variety of expressive voices: music, sculpture, writing, and dance. My work has been anthologized in *Positively Gay, Lesbians at Midlife: The Creative Transition, Blood Whispers, She Who Was Lost Is Remembered, Riding Desire, The Poetry of Sex, Indivisible: New Short Fiction by West Coast Gay and Lesbian Writers*, and *In A Different Light*. I have also published essays, book reviews, and news articles in a diverse spectrum of publications.

I write about and celebrate the erotic in lesbian life as a conscious antidote to the toxic despair and bitterness that sometimes poisons my spirit and would numb me into apathy. It is an essential element in the maintenance of both my personal well-being and my political consciousness. Initially, I was afraid to even approach this subject, but I have come to savor the pleasure of the erotic in literature, both that which I create and that created by others.

La Verne Gagehabib I am a Black/American born July 26, 1945 in Houston, Texas. My family moved to Berkeley, California when I was eight years of age. I grew up in the Bay Area. I enlisted into the Women's Army Corps, (WAC) after high school and spent eight years on active duty. In 1971, I returned to the South Bay Area, San Jose, California, where I met my life mate.

My partner of 13 years, our four cats and two dogs presently live in the Northwest. While attending the University in pursuit of a PH.D in Sociology, I am working toward starting my own publishing/Video production business called Her Thang. I enjoy reading and writing stories about Lesbians during the western times. Having completed a trilogy about a small Lesbian community of women in 1867, I am looking for a publisher.

This story, "My Buddy," was created from a fantasy story that ran through my mind as a tease to a friend. It has no relevance to my relationship or life. It's just a story.

Elissa Goldberg I am a reader and a writer – of stories, of recipes, of life. Two of my favorite occupations are listening and staring. I continue to hone those skills by working as a social worker.

With this story, "Peppermint Candy," I wanted to talk about doors, and how they keep closing and opening all through our lives, even into old age. With a death, one door closing, comes sadness – as well as the wonder of it all, which only opens other doors. It's what's behind those opening doors that's always – in one way or another – erotic.

Barbara Herrera is a Jewish Cuban-American single mother of a son and two daughters. A homebirth midwife in Orlando, Florida, she helps women touch the fire within – the fire that warms, the fire that heals, the fire that transforms. She's also a *really big* Big Pants Woman and loves it! Her favorite tattoo on her right breast says, "I am a Woman Giving Birth to Myself." And she is.

She is the author of the erotic collection *Seasons of Erotic Love* (1992).

K.Linda Kivi: born June 25, 1962. I was born and raised in the Estonian refugee community in Toronto. Three years ago, I moved to rural B.C. where I currently live, write and serve my cat. Writer's workshops and writer's groups have been essential in my development as a writer. I've published one non-fiction book, *Canadian Women Making Music* (Green Dragon Press, 1992) and numerous short stories in journals and anthologies across North America, including Sinister Wisdom, Common Lives/Lesbian Lives, *Sister/Stranger*. My first novel, *If Home is a Place*, will be published by Polestar Press in 1995 and I'm looking for a publisher for my collection of lesbian sex stories.

Why Sex Writing is Important: For me, writing about sex is about saying yes, not just to my fantasies, but to my fundamental animal self. It's about surfacing, discovering and affirming lesbian sexual realities, whatever they may be, as survivors or not, and moving forward from there. It's about sharing possibilities. Sex writing is about my place in the wilderness. It's about becoming whole and thereby acquiring the power to change the world.

Sandra Lambert Born a military brat on June 7, 1952 to an English mother and a father from West Virginia, I moved every few years until 1969. I spent the next twenty years in Georgia, going to college, coming out, getting sober, and ending a short career as a physician's assistant to work for eight years in a feminist bookstore. As a baby I had polio and used braces and crutches all my life until 1988 when the effects of post polio syndrome made using a wheelchair, and now an electric scooter, a better choice for mobility. In 1989 I retired and moved to Gainesville, Florida where I am trying to learn how to relax. I have been writing since 1986 and have had poetry, fiction, essays, and interviews published in various lesbian periodicals and books.

There seems to be this dichotomy in lesbian writing about sex. It can either be really hot steamy stuff where no one is allowed to have any problems and everything just "flows," or else its all about "the struggle" to "overcome" past abuse. I personally benefit immensely from both of these types of writing, but my real life is an ever changing mixture of the two and I've tried to write that. But does it work? Can you write a graphic, lusty scene that you want to pass the wet test with your readers and still include the oppressions of daily life and the shadows of past atrocities?

Kate Berne Miller I was born March 12th, 1954 in New York City. I was adopted at three months and grew up in Rhode Island, where the state bird is a chicken. I am mixed-blood Cherokee/Irish and live in a low-income housing collective in Seattle, Wa. I work at Red and Black Books, also a collective. Being different in the world I grew up in (adopted, Indian and lesbian), has been educational for me.

I think erotic writing is important for several reasons. As lesbians (and even just as women), it is important for us to define and celebrate our own sexuality. For me personally, sex is a language, another way of communicating, and I couldn't write about relationships without including sexuality. I couldn't write about nature without including erotica either.

Ruth Mountaingrove Having attained the age of 70, I wonder what's next? I started as a poet and a photographer and to that I added songwriting and singing, painting and short story writing along with some community work. (I produce both programs for both the local radio and the television station.) My recent work has been in the quarterly *Writing For Our Lives*, and four anthologies: *Write From The Heart*, *All Our Secrets Exposed*, *The Poetry Of Sex*, and *Paper Only*. I also write reviews and articles for the *L - Word*, our local news letter in Humboldt county. I live in Arcata, California.

In "Almost A Love Story," I touch on that very delicate place where friendship and the erotic blur or blend, depending on how you look at it. Where is the line where friendship crosses over into sexuality? If there is no genital sex, does that mean the friends are not lovers? I would like to see more lesbian writers explore this country.

Paula Neves I was born into a family of Portuguese immigrants on 5/7/68 in the Ironbound section of Newark. I grew up in the Newark area and currently live in central NJ. I have a B.A. in English and Portuguese from Rutgers University, where I am an English/writing tutor. My writing has appeared in *The Poetry of Sex* and *The Portuguese Heritage Journal*. I contribute monthly feature articles and a story series to *The Network*, NJ's gay and lesbian magazine. Additionally, a story of mine about lesbian parenting will be included in a parenting anthology being put out by a Boston collective sometime late this or early next year.

Inevitably, my writing often reflects the balance and conflict between cultural identity and sexual identity because these issues are so pertinent to my own experience. The eroticism comes out of that tension, even though it is probably certain that these two will either meet or that the culture will have to be pushed aside. I hope they meet.

Lesléa Newman (Brooklyn, NY 1955) is the author of 16 books for adults and children, including *Heather Has Two Mommies, Sweet Dark Places, In Every Laugh A Tear, Saturday is Pattyday, A Letter To Harvey Milk,* and *SomeBODY To Love.* "I think writing about sexuality is important simply because it is part of who we are. Writing about women's sexuality is especially important as a way to demystify, correct misinformation, and celebrate the passion and excitement of our lives."

Berté Ramirez I am an artist and writer living in the Bay Area. I am half-Puerto Rican and half-Filipino and was raised in southern California without much of my cultural heritage around me. I have a degree in Fine Art and an interest in writing and photography.

I study sex and intimacy partly because as an artist it is in my nature to do so and partly because as a woman my sexuality has been co-opted to serve man and his society. I want to reclaim my body and my sexuality so that I can be more truly who I am and love truly as I was meant to love.

Shelley Rachor I am a 48 year old Portuguese-German sexplorer in the process of redefining my sexuality. My formal education ended with my junior year in high school. I then began learning at an accelerated rate in the classrooms of the hearts of the women I have loved. Their brilliant and creative imaginations have been the inspiration for discovery of the art and knowledge within myself. Their collective minds are an elite encyclopedia with each volume a special course of study.

When I read erotica, I fantasize about the author, not the characters. When I write about sex, I fantasize about the reader. I want her to fantasize about me. There is no greater excitement than knowing a woman is touching herself while my words look on.

Janet Silverstein was born Feb. 4, 1955 in Brooklyn, N.Y., grew up on Long Island and went to college in Buffalo, N.Y. (where I discovered that one's nostrils can truly freeze together). I've been published in *Common Lives/Lesbian Lives, Advanced Warning* and *Fiction Forum.*

I seem to be writing about sexuality out of my own need to give my fantasies free rein and to learn how to remove my internal editor. When the computer didn't explode and my mother didn't emerge from the screen waggling her finger at me the first time I typed the word "clit", I got the message that it was an okay thing to do. In the process I discovered I rather enjoyed it as well.

Susan Stinson (10/17/60, Amarillo, Texas) grew up in the suburbs of Denver. Her first novel, with a working title of *Fat Girl Dances with Rocks*, will be published in Fall 1994 by Spinsters, Ink. "Milk" is an excerpt from her second novel, *Martha Moody*. She is a member of Valley Lesbian Writers Group, has received support from the Vogelstein and Wurlitzer Foundations, and been a featured performer at the conference of the National Association to Advance Fat Acceptance. She lives in Easthampton, MA.

"I write about sex because words first pulled me through their sensuality: their shapes, the way they feel in my mouth. I'm fat, and burned for years for women who couldn't see the erotic charge of my swells and folds. This has changed, but I want to be visible to other fat women – here we are – complex, wanton, lifting belly, loved. I also love the power of compression and of nuance; I can be changed forever by a single motion of the tongue."

Pearl Time'sChild was a 1940 baby who grew up to build a house, drive a car, sew, and write - all those things it was so fun to pretend she was doing when she was little. As a child, she had never heard of getting a PhD, or she might have pretended that, too. Time'sChild now teaches college, under a different name. She has published in both women's movement and academic journals, most recently, a set of pieces in the lesbian-focus issue of Haptia.

She writes: "However pleasurable it may be, the erotic can also be a lonely place if we do not have the words to talk about it, or are not allowed to say them. I write to break silences long imposed. I write to know myself. And to be known, to answer the calls of the other brave women who write the erotic down."

Chea Villanueva is half Filipino and half Irish and believes this combination of strong cultures has helped make her what she is today. Much of her writing is based on people, places, and situations she has encountered in her own life. She is the author of *The Girlfriends Trilogy*, and her poems and short stories have appeared in *The Persistent Desire*, *The Poetry of Sex*, *Making Waves*, *Riding Desire*, *Matrix*, and *Common Lives/Lesbian Lives*. She is 41 years old and lives in San Francisco.

Heidi Zednik I was born in Miami, Florida in 1965 to an American mother and an Austrian father. A few years after my birth we moved to Austria, which became my primary residence until the age of 15, at which time I then returned to the states.

I began writing poetry and short stories in my early teens, but instead of pursuing writing I fell in love with painting my senior year in college. I ditched all former intentions of becoming a translator and concentrated solely on painting. In 1990 I received my M.F.A. in painting from the University of North Carolina at Chapel Hill with my focus being the interaction of visual images with text and word-images.

In the fall of 1991 I unexpectedly fell madly in love and began writing again, especially erotic poetry. Returning to words I found I could voice precisely WHAT I wanted to say, whereas with painting I had largely expressed abstractions. My lover and I have since moved to San Francisco, and due to space and changing environments I've shifted primarily to writing. Even though I've exhibited nationally I find the visuals need a rest now; I've other things to say.